The Shade
Of The Trees

THE SHADE
OF THE TREES

A NARRATIVE
BASED ON THE LIFE AND CAREER
OF
LIEUTENANT GENERAL
THOMAS JONATHAN "STONEWALL" JACKSON

Jack I. Brown

Todd & Honeywell, Inc.

Copyright © 1988 by Jack I. Brown
First Edition

Published by Todd & Honeywell, Inc./Ten Cuttermill Road/
Great Neck, New York 11021

Library of Congress Cataloging-in-Publication Data

Brown, Jack I., 1915-
    The shade of the trees / Jack I. Brown.
        p.   cm.
    ISBN 0-89962-665-3
    1. Jackson, Stonewall, 1824-1863—Fiction.   2. United States-
-History—Civil War, 1861-1865—Fiction.   I. Title.
PS3552.R685627S5   1988
813' .54—dc 19   88-20184
                                                                              CIP

Manufactured in the United States of America

Contents

DEDICATION

To My Dearest Celia, Now and Always!

ACKNOWLEDGEMENTS

I am deeply grateful to the following persons, institutions, libraries, museums, universities and archives for the help given me in compiling the research in writing this book. No author can successfully write any type book unless he not only digs out the information but must rely on the knowledge passed on to him by others. Besides the regular information so necessary for compiling a book such as "The Shade of the Trees," there are other supportive factors which the author acknowledges at this time in the following listing:

Alling, Charlene: Curator of MSS and Archives, Brockenbrough Library, Museum of the Confederacy, Richmond, VA

Baird, Nancy: Historian and Writer, Paris, VA

Baker, Don: Historian and Playwright, Lime Kiln Arts, Lexington, VA

Barksdale, Colonel Flournoy H.: Historian, Lexington, VA

Bell, Jr., Stewart: Historian and Writer, Winchester, VA

Blue & Gray Magazine: Columbus, OH

Boren, Senator David L.: Oklahoma Senator, Washington, D.C.

Brooks, Jr., L.A.: President, Civil War Roundtable, Waynesboro, VA

Brown, Celia L: Research Assistant, Tulsa, OK

Brown, Dr. Jay Louis: Research Assistant, Dallas, TX

Brown, Dr. Richard L.: Research Assistant, Dallas, TX

Brown, Dr. Katharine L.: Executive Director, Woodrow Wilson Birthplace, Staunton, VA

Civil War Series: Time and Life Books, Alexandria, VA

Civil War Times Magazine: Harrisburg, PA

Coit Collection Civil War Papers: Mills College, Oakland, CA

Comess, Linda B.: Research Assistant, Plano, TX

Confederacy, Museum Of The: Richmond, VA

Confederate Museum: New Orleans, LA

Cunningham, June: Director, VMI Museum, Jackson Memorial Hall, Lexington, VA

Denison, Colonel Stanley L.: Waynesboro, VA

Drake, Mrs. Ann: Tulsa, OK

Frye, Dennis E.: Historian, Harper's Ferry, National Historical Park, Harper's Ferry, West VA

Gallaher, William B.: Writer and Historian, Waynesboro, VA

Gilmore, Margaret B.: Clerk of the City Council, Waynesboro, VA

Gussman, Mr. & Mrs. Herbert: Tulsa, OK

Hadsel, Mrs. Fred L.: Historian and Lecturer,
Lexington, VA

Harman, Joe: Writer, Staunton, VA

Hassler, Dr. William: Historian and Writer,
Winchester, VA

Hennessy, John J.: Historian and Writer, Manassas
National Historical Park, Manassas, VA

Jacob, Diane B.: Archivest-VMI, Archives/Special Collections Dept.,
Lexington, VA

James, Larry: Historian, Fredericksburg and Spotsylvania
National Military Park, Fredericksburg, VA

Jennings, Mrs. Pat: Director, Stonewall Jackson House,
Winchester, VA

Krick, Robert K.: Chief Historian and Author,
Fredericksburg and Spotsylvania, National Military Park
Fredericksburg, VA

Lexington Presbyterian Church: Lexington, VA

Library of Congress: Washington, D.C.

Louisiana Historical Association: New Orleans, LA

Louisiana State University: Baton Rouge, LA

Lynn, Michael Anne: Director, Stonewall Jackson House,
Lexington, VA

Marder, Dr. Daniel: Professor and Author, University
of Tulsa, Tulsa, OK

McAfee, Jim: Great-Great-Grandson of General Jackson,
Annandale, VA

McFarlin Library: University of Tulsa Special Collection,
Tulsa, OK

Merchant, Dr. J. Holt: Associate Professor of History
Washington and Lee University, Lexington, VA

Mertz, Craig: Historian, Guinea Station National Park,
Guinea, VA

Military Archives Division, National Archives and Records:
Military Service Branch, Washington, D.C.

Morris, Mrs. Ruth: Tulsa, OK

National Archives Trust Fund Board: Washington, D.C.

Pfanz, Donald C.: Historian, Petersburg National Battlefield,
Petersburg, VA

Phillips, Geraldine N.: Chief, Military Service Branch,
Military Archives Division, National Archives,
Washington, D.C.

Pusey III, Dr. William W.: Researcher, Dean and Professor
Emeritus, University Library Special Collections,
Washington and Lee University, Lexington, VA

Rice, Dr. Lawrence D.: Secretary Treasurer, Louisiana
Historical Association, New Orleans, LA

Reinbold, Dorothy: Librarian, Waynesboro Public Library
Waynesboro, VA

Russell, Jerry: Civil War Roundtable Lecturer, Society of
Civil War Historians, Little Rock, AR

San Francisco Public Library: Main Library Special Collections,
San Francisco, CA

Shrader, Colonel Charles R.: Chief, Historical Services Division, The Chief of Military History and the Center of Military History Washington, D.C.

Sisler, Dr. Jerry: Civil War Historian—Mississippi, Tulsa, OK

Stonewall Jackson House Museum: Lexington, VA

Stonewall Jackson House Museum: Winchester, VA

Strong, Dr. Edwin: Professor and Writer, University of Tulsa, Tulsa, OK

Stuart, Harold C.: Great-Grand Nephew of Major General J.E.B. "Jeb" Stuart; Attorney and Big Game Hunter, Tulsa, OK

Sublett, John W.: Attorney and Historian, Tulsa, OK

Sutro Library Civil War Papers: San Francisco State University, San Francisco, CA

Tanner, Robert G.: Attorney and Author, Atlanta, GA

Tulsa Public Library—Main: Tulsa, OK

United States Military Academy: Archives-Department of the Army, West Point, New York

University of Tennessee: Library Publications Section, Knoxville, TN

University of Texas: Library Publications Section, Austin, TX

University of Tulsa: Main Library, Tulsa, OK

University of Virginia: Main Library, Charlottesville, VA

Virginia Country Magazine: Middleburg, VA

Virginia Military Institute: Lexington, VA

Washington and Lee University: Main Library Manuscript Collection, Lexington, VA

Watts, Dabney: City Councillor and Attorney, Historian, Winchester, VA

Zuckerman, Mayor Charles M.: Winchester, VA

Author's Note

In writing this narrative based on the life and career of one of the outstanding Americans of the Civil War period, Lieutenant General Thomas Jonathan (Stonewall) Jackson, I have utilized a fictional person, Caleb Joshua Sparks to best portray the events and period covered from birth to death of our immortal hero. By using such a method, I hopefully have stayed away from any and all arguments from that group of readers who will look with every means available for either contradiction or refutation of statements made.

Everyone knows that the facts of history do not change. Only those who attempt to interpret history to their own liking, or who try to explain away the facts as they occurred, will take exception to the statements made concerning decisions of General Jackson and the actual battles that took place in which our hero played such a vital role.

This book was written for the enjoyment and information of the general public and to enlighten them as much as possible about the time in our national history when the country was torn apart by Civil War, and when immortal heroes like Stonewall Jackson rose to the occasion. Naturally, a book based on Jackson's life and career should cover primarily the high as well as the low points. You can't go into the most minute detail without boring people.

In order to establish scenery and background for the story, it was necessary to create certain fictional characters as well as suitable fictional events based on word-of-mouth stories, legends, true incidents and some little-known facts. Therefore, in certain instances, the reader will learn of some things which the majority of history books dealing with Jackson and the Civil War do not mention, and certainly are not portrayed as fact.

On the other hand, the recitation by the narrator, Caleb Joshua Sparks, of the events of battle, delineates factual history as told by him as he saw it and does not necessarily tie in with the most detailed military reports as submitted by the writers of the various texts written on the history of the Civil War.

General Jackson was a very complex person. To explain him and his life career to the public is not an easy task. In composing the narrative, the author has taken certain literary license without distorting the story to one that would make the great Jackson appear to be anything that he actually wasn't. The times, the events, the people with whom he associated, but most of all, the man himself, created the persona around whom "The Shade of the Trees" was written. The young school child, the high school student, the college or university enrollee, the working person, the banker, the politician, the educated as well as the uneducated are entitled to know Jackson's story and the role he played on the American stage of history. If in some small way I have reached a good many of these people and given them a better understanding of Stonewall Jackson and the permanent place he has earned in the history of our country, then I will feel amply rewarded for the years of research and study spent in gathering the information and sharing it with my fellow Americans. One final word, however...

Jackson was considered by military experts of the nineteenth century as one of the greatest strategists since Napoleon. The Battle of Chancellorsville was the most brilliant Confederate achievement of the War. The renowned historian and biographer, Colonel George F. R. Henderson called the "defeat of 130,000 men by 60,000, the tactical masterpiece of the nineteenth century."

The Battle of Gettysburg was the high watermark and turning point of the Civil War and military authorities have differed on any influence Jackson might have had on the outcome had he lived and participated. At Gettysburg, the tactical situation actually required the ability and peculiar genius of a Jackson for swift and bold flank movements. General Lee who never committed a rash judgment said: "If I had had Jackson at Gettysburg, I should have won the battle, and a complete victory there would have resulted in the establishment of Southern independence." Thus fate which followed Jackson during his lifetime sealed the doom at Gettysburg of the Southern cause!

Jack I. Brown
August 31, 1987

Author in front of Jackson statue
at V.M.I. campus

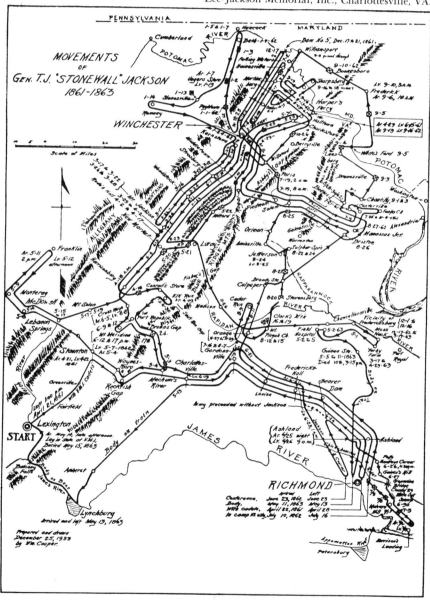

Map of "Stonewall" Jackson's movements.

Prologue

Permit me to introduce myself. I am Caleb Joshua Sparks, born in Forestville, Virginia in 1819. As a boy and later as a man, I was known as "C.J." to my family and friends. My childhood was a happy one filled with pleasant memories of parents and a large family of brothers and sisters.

When I was eighteen, I joined the United States Army as a volunteer and served through the Mexican War in the Field Artillery. It was during this time that I met Lieutenant Thomas Jonathan Jackson, a recent Artillery graduate of West Point.

It was not long after our first meeting that I determined that Lieutenant Jackson was marked for greatness and knew that our lives were destined to be inexorably bound together. I sensed that every effort would have to be made by me to learn as much about him as I could. He was an enigmatic individual, quite religious, somewhat mystic, strictly honest, fearless, and had, apparently, resolved to make the military his lifetime work.

There was no way of knowing that fate had already determined that I would serve with him until his untimely death following his greatest military triumph, at the Battle of Chancellorsville, Virginia in May of 1863!

When Jackson died and was laid to rest at Lexington, Virginia, I returned to my quarters pondering the loss of my personal friend and leader. I began to realize that one of the greatest men in our American history had left an indelible imprint on the South as well as the United States of America. He loved Virginia, had an unshakeable belief in his Heavenly Father, and fought for the Confederate cause in which he believed. There were few men left who could emulate his miltiary achievements and I knew that I would have to write the story of his life and career.

Fortunatley, I kept a log of most of the events which occurred during the time I served with General Jackson and it is from this personal record, talks with many of his staff officers, friends and others close to him that I composed this narrative.

Chapter 1

"What are the thoughts that are stirring his breast?
What is the mystical vision he sees?
Let us pass over the river and rest
Under the shade of the trees!
Caught the high psalm of ecstatic delight,
Heard the harps singing like sounding of seas;
Saw earth's pure-hearted one, walking in white,
Under the shade of the trees!
Surely for him it was well...it was best...
War worn, yet asking no furlough of ease,
There to pass over the river, and rest
Under the shade of the trees!"

My most vivid memory of Stonewall Jackson was the time we marched to Winchester. It was January 1862 and the country was in the midst of one of the coldest winters Virginia had ever known. Snow mixed with sleet and ice came down so heavily one might have felt that even heaven conspired against the footsore and hungry Confederate Army as they struggled toward a haven from the elements.

Not even a bird flew above. If there were any forest creatures alive, they were not seen. The wind joined ranks with the bitter cold and each breath of frozen air reminded the veterans of their many battles to the death, when fatigue and weariness edged each of them to a near state of collapse. The more they marched and struggled through the snow and ice, the more discouraged they became.

The soldiers were covered with blankets and old rags around their faces and necks. Their legs had little covering to ward off the cold and many suffered from frostbite. Hoary frost covered their eyebrows and beards while ice hung from their rifles and bedrolls. Face and finger skin froze as water on a pond. There were many who did not have enough protection and dropped by the wayside only to freeze to death. The line of march could not be halted for roadside burials, so the dead soldiers were loaded on supply wagons for later interment in Winchester.

The stillness of the forest was marked only by the sound of an army making its way through the snow covered paths and unmarked frozen roads that intersected the solid wall of heavily ice laden pines. The ground shook and trees trembled as the pounding of men's feet, horses' hooves and heavy wheels of artillery caissons marched and rolled in a crescendo of military symphony.

The pots, pans, and kettles rattled against the sides of the supply wagons as they lurched and groaned while the heavy draft horses struggled to keep pace with the long column of officers and soldiers of the Army of the Shenandoah with Major General Thomas Jonathan ''Stonewall'' Jackson commanding. They were on their way to winter quarters in the Winchester, Virginia area.

Jackson realized the proximity of the opposing Union army and urged his men on to the Winchester haven with the utmost speed. Weary and worn down from the constant fighting up and down the Valley of the Shenandoah, the brilliant Jackson was bringing his valiant and superb army of veteran fighters to a well earned rest.

Jackson, the ''soldiers' soldier,'' beloved by his men and honored by the acclaim of his Southern compatriots, respected and feared by his Northern enemies, rode at the head of his troops. He sat erect in the saddle with full beard encased in ice, his snow covered forage cap draped over his forehead and legs in ''Old Sorrel's'' stirrups. His sword dangled at his side and his gauntlet covered hands held the sleet covered reins. An India rubber cape was draped over him to provide some warmth and dryness on the grueling march.

''Foward, men! Yonder is Winchester. Hot food and rest awaits us there,'' he cried, as he rode up and down the lines encouraging his men to press on with every ounce of remaining strength.

The men bent forward in one last effort to force their feet into the cadence of the marching army. Despite the high morale in the ranks, bodily discomfort and hunger began to take its toll. Jackson realized the Army of the Shenandoah was near its breaking point. Only the strong, rigid "Stonewall" stood between his men and open rebellion.

He summoned his aide, Henry Kyd Douglas and told him, "Captain, pass the order to all brigades that Winchester and its environs will be our winter bivouac. We shall be there presently. All other commanders report to me for allocation of quarters for men and horses. Warm food and hot coffee will be prepared upon arrival at our new base."

"Yes sir, General, at once!" Douglas answered.

Jackson nodded and added, "Captain, you will see to it that all regimental commanders provide for the sick and wounded first and provide burial details for the dead, as soon as possible!"

Was it any wonder that the men of the Shenandoah army respected and loved their "Old Jack" or "Old Blue Light" as many were want to call him? His concern for their welfare and well being was always uppermost in mind!

General Jackson, tired and somewhat shaken by the ague, but resolute in his determination to bring his men safely into the haven of winter quarters, looked heavenward and raised his arm high above his head. For a moment, the line of men wavered and almost stopped in its forward motion but the General's aides recognized this gesture as a prayer, rather than a command, and waved the column forward. Jackson had just asked his Heavenly Father for guidance and safety in bringing his men in with utmost speed.

"Stonewall" urged his horse forward at a faster pace and his men followed. They had gathered strength from Jackson's prayer and thoughts of burning camp fires and hot food spurred them on. They longed for a place to lie down and rest and realized they had to have shelter soon for another snow storm was building up. Jackson stopped to pray for Divine intercession in holding off the storm until he could get his men to Winchester by nightfall.

We finally reached Winchester where most of the army bivouacked with the General; another section marched to Bath and the remainder set out for Moorefield. At last Jackson's Army of the Shenandoah was safe in its winter quarters.

All of us who survived the march, knew it was because of the General's leadership and experience that we had made it thorugh the storm. The army realized why Jackson was so successful in all of his military undertakings. He was a strict disciplinarian, doing his duty, always at his post as Commander, expecting and demanding the same of every man who served under him. Enforcement of discipline was a cardinal principle in Jackson's field command. He would have his own men shot for violation of the military code or for the slightest infringement of commands which appeared to be trivial to most soldiers.

He insisted that the Army must condition itself so the forbearance, privation and lack of the niceties of civilian life were to be accepted as a normal way of Army routine. He demanded that every order issued must be implicitly obeyed. Violation was subject to court martial proceedings with death by shooting as the ultimate penalty. An Army must have order and its enforcement was necessary so that discipline was maintained to avoid chaos and defeat on the battlefield. Jackson's men experienced and never forgot the stern but necessary lesson!

Chapter 2

Thomas Jackson was born in the rugged and tough mountain country of Clarksburg, Virginia, on January 21, 1824. His father's name was Jonathan Jackson, born in 1790 and his mother's maiden name was Julia Beckwith Neale, born in 1798. Jonathan practiced law in Clarksburg and involved himself with his neighbors in the affairs of the community. The Jacksons had four children: Elizabeth, Warren, Thomas and Laura. The oldest, Elizabeth, died when she was seven.

Life in the mountains was not easy. Far removed from the larger cities of the Eastern coast of the country and somewhat isolated from the rest of the world, the people of Clarksburg experienced daily life as a challenge. Survival and continuity were the two musts of the mountain population. Making a living by dint of hard work was an accepted fact of life for most of the mountaineers. That these people were born to persevere was no idle statement or exaggeration of fact. They were hard working, God fearing, honest and resolute pioneers who loved their country and their native state. They were not beholden to anyone and bent their knee only to Almighty God!

The Jackson house was built on a large tract of land and was made of rough hewn logs with the cracks filled with clay to give protection from the cold and rain. Wood shingles covered the home. Two large chimneys, one at either end of the house, held stone fireplaces which were used to heat the rooms and cook their food. Large iron pots swung from hooks over the fireplace and there Julia prepared their meals. She would bake their bread in a black skillet which sat on a trivet in the smouldering coals, make stew, cook meat in the pots and serve the family on a rough hewn log table.

Life was hard for the Jacksons, for Jonathan, although a good attorney, was no businessman. He was generous and helpful to his friends, often to a fault. He would endorse notes and loan money out without security and when the amounts were not repaid, he would become personally liable and eventually lost everything. Julia and the family had to make do with very little and if it was not for the farm, they would have starved!

The children helped all they could. They worked a garden, did the chores, milked a cow and helped as much as possible. Julia canned the surplus vegetables and stored the potatoes, carrots and other garden products in their root bin. She made butter for their use and often sold eggs, cheese and cream to neighbors. She would take the money and buy flour, meal and sugar. Soon this became their only source of income as her husband weakened and could not work at all.

Julia was pregnant and heavy with child the day Jonathan died. It was March 26, 1826, and the next day Laura Ann was born. The next four years were the worst the family could remember. Julia tried to bring the children up by herself but finally gave up and married another attorney, Captain Blake B. Woodson of Clarksburg. They soon moved to Fayette County, Virginia. Tom and Laura lived with them for a short while but they were not happy. Eventually they moved to their their Grandmother Jackson's home.

It was not long before the children were left orphaned. Julia died in 1831 and their grandmother passed away shortly thereafter. The three children went to live with their Uncle Cummins at Jackson's Mill in Lewis County, Virginia. Tom was just seven years old when he found that he would be faced with a new life. Although he had been brought up on a small farm, he learned that his Uncle owned a very large place which was south of Clarksburg. There was a grist mill and a sawmill on the confluence of West Fork and Freeman's Creek owned by their Uncle Cummins. There would be lots to learn!

Cummins taught Tom and Warren everything about the farm and mills. The other interst of Cummins was horse racing. It was a popular pastime and business for people in the area. Tom became his Uncle's jockey and was taught the fine art of racing; when to let the horse go at full speed and when to ride him slowly. Young Tom learned to ride erect in the saddle and how to handle a horse, an asset which came in handy later on in life!

Young Jackson must have come into the world with a sense of honesty. He took his work seriously and tried to learn everything about farm life, working every day, even at a young age, doing his part to earn his keep. He helped cut down trees, hitched teams to drag the logs to the mill, worked in the fields in spring and summer and lent a hand with most of the chores.

He liked to draw the sap from maple trees and would always help as the men boiled it down to make syrup. Uncle Cummins soon found out that he could trust the youngster to do whatever chore was needed and above all, could count on him to tell the truth.

The slaves on the farm would work in the fields, while others worked in the house. Sheep were sheared each spring and one of the slaves would wash the wool, then card and weave it into homespun cloth. From this, the women would make the homespun clothes everyone wore. The coarse cloth was sometimes hot and scratchy but it was sturdy and provided clothing which could stand up to the heavy work on the farm. Much of Tom's education came from watching the slaves work.

The water from the creek held a great fascination for Tom and Warren. After the day's work was done, they would slip off to the banks for fishing or take a swim in the cool, clear water. They liked to swim to the other side and lie down on the bank in the shade of the trees. Often, Tom went there to rest and enjoy the quiet. He liked to think about things and plan for the future.

I remember one particular story they told about Tom that impressed me. It seems he liked to fish and was good at it. He contracted with Conrad Kester, a neighbor, to sell all the fish he caught, over a foot in length, for fifty cents each. One day he caught a particularly fine Pike, about three feet long, which attracted much attention. As he brought it in to town, one of the neighbors said to him, "That's a pretty fine fish you have there, Tom. I'd like to buy it." Without evidencing any interest in what the neighbor said, Tom unhestitatingly replied, "It's sold to Mr. Kester." When the man tried to tempt Tom by offering him a larger sum than Mr. Kester would pay, young Jackson glared at him and said, "If you want any part of this fish, you'll have to deal with its owner, Mr. Kester!"

When Kester saw the fish, he was taken with its large size and offered Jackson more than the fifty cents they previously had agreed on. "No sir," replied Tom, "I will not take any more than what we agreed on since you did pay me for some that were smaller at fifty cents each!"

Thus the transaction was closed and young Tom took pride in that he had kept his word and strengthened his integrity by the incident. This was just another indication of character building in the life of a growing young man destined for greatness and marking time before striding forth on the stage of history! Little did he know or realize that he was preparing for the fierce struggles which awaited him in his future eventful career!

This incident in Tom's early life was one of a series of character building experiences which molded together to establish within him a personality of direct dealing with any undertaking. In the years that followed, the boy began creating the man we so loved and admired!

Uncle Cummins took Tom along on some of his fishing and hunting trips and taught him how to handle a line, set traps, catch rabbits by snares and how to set and fire a gun. They developed a mutual liking for each other. The young man learned to appreciate the farm and the community. He met some friends his own age who enjoyed playing games, swimming, fishing, the great outdoors, and a host of other activities. He and his friends discussed the topics of the day with the major subject being that of slavery. He often expressed his views on the subject and told his friends that he felt sorry for the blacks and their situation as slaves.

Warren and Tom talked about visiting Uncle Cummins' brother, Henry. He lived on Neales Island in the Ohio River about four miles above Parkersburg. Arrangements were made for them to go down the Ohio and Mississippi Rivers and spend the winter near the southwest corner of Kentucky. They chopped and sold wood to be burned in the boilers of the river boats. They stayed with Uncle Henry for a while but found that the humidity and the climate were bad for Warren's asthma. He came down with a fever so as soon as he recovered, they went back to Uncle Cummins. Warren never did recover from his ailment and died in November of 1841.

Young Jackson went to school whenever lessons were taught. There was no teacher available in that remote area but from time to time one would come and teach the children of the general community. It was hard to keep a teacher because the residents were not able to financially support one. Tom found that he learned slowly but remembered everything about the things that interested him most. He spent as much time as he could spare in studying his lessons and reading books. He never lost track of the fact that whatever he hoped to achieve in life would have to be done by himself, no matter how difficult it might be. His mother, father, and Uncle Cummins had planted the seeds of life in him and had given him a philosophy and pragmatic creed which just waited for growth and development!

By the time he entered his teens, his character was formed. It was plain to see that he had developed some solid axioms such as honesty, integrity, decency, completion of matters once started and obedience of established law and self-discipline. He believed that one should set a code of procedure and adhere to it. Thus, from thinking and rationalizing, Jackson gradually developed his life motto: "You may be whatever you resolve to be."

Jackson enrolled at Colonel Alexander Scott Withers school in January of 1839 and completed his formal education by the age of sixteen. He became a teacher and taught in a one room school which was rudimentary in every way. He was very strict with the children and never allowed any moments of relaxation. The students improved their penmanship but little else, for Jackson was not a good teacher. The parents and school trustees were not happy with his work so after a period of four months, he was out of a job.

Uncle Cummins was ever on the lookout for Tom's welfare. He walked up to Tom one day and said, "Tom, I heard that a job for Constable will be open soon. Why don't you run for it and see if you can be elected? You'd be a good one!"

"That's a right good idea, Uncle. I'd shore like to be a Constable, but I don't know much about politics."

"Don't worry about that, boy. I know some people who can help you. Just let me work on it for awhile and we'll see."

Uncle Cummins dressed up one day in his frock tailed coat and top hat, got in his buggy and made a trip to the county seat. He paid a visit to some of his cronies and presented them with the idea of his nephew running for constable. Before the day was over, he had gained enough support to make it worth while for the young man. He thanked the men and returned to tell Tom the good news.

"Nephew, it's all set! My friends say they'll support you. In fact they were very complimentary of you and your standing in the community. Said they need some young blood to help keep the community in line."

"Thank you, Uncle. I'll get to work and draw up a plan. I'll need your help when it comes to the speech making. You'll have to rehearse me on what to say."

"Don't worry about that part of it. I'll help you and so will the others!"

Tom did not realize that the trip his uncle made to town was to call in a few political debts from his friends. Cummins had been a powerful political figure in the community for a long time and had done a lot of people favors. Now he was out to collect. They were happy to repay him.

Young Jackson ran for Constable and was elected. He took office in June of 1841 at the age of seventeen. His principal work was to try to collect debts. He found that he was good at it but didn't like the practices he had to use to get the funds. It rubbed against his conscience when he had to employ some shoddy or shady methods to outwit the debtors. His principles of honesty and directness were being compromised. Tom felt guilty and soon knew that he could not keep on with such a job. He resolved to stick if out for a year, then after that required time, would begin to search for a position which was more to his liking. He needed a job which would be challenging yet suitable for the standards which he had set for himself.

He didn't mention his plans to the uncle who had worked so hard to help him get elected realizing that everything he was or would be was due to the influence of this relative who had become his benefactor. Tom would not do hurt or do anything to displease him, and decided to bide his time and wait for just the right opportunity.

Uncle Cummins was proud of him and the way he was developing into such a responsible citizen. Laura and Tom had become very dear to Uncle, and he devoted much of his time to their development. Little did he realize that fate would soon intervene in Tom's career plans!

In the early part of 1842, Congressman Samuel Hays announced that his District of Virginia would be entitled to an appointment for a vacancy at the United States Military Academy in West Point, New York. Any candidate who was accepted would be given a four year education free and an opportunity for a career in the United States Army, if he qualified and graduated from the Academy.

This announcement elated Tom Jackson. He felt it was fate knocking at his door because he saw his chance to get an education without having to worry about the cost. He knew there were other candidates from the district, including Gibson Butcher.

Tom knew his education was a poor one and equal perhaps to completion of the lower grades in the school system. However, there was a point in his favor. The other candidates did not have any better education than he did. All of the men took the examination and when it was concluded, Gibson Butcher won out. He went on to West Point but did not stay long. He came back home disappointed in the Academy. He had refused to buckle down to saluting, drilling, performing certain duties, following the schedules and keeping his uniform in order. He hated to spend the time in classes studying foreign languages, science, earth structures and other subjects. Butcher came to Jackson and told him he had quit and the place would be open in the class if Tom wanted to try for it.

Jackson was overcome with joy at a second chance. He vowed not to let anything stand in the way this time. He went to see his Uncle and said, "Uncle, Gibson Butcher came to see me today and told me that he was leaving West Point."

"What in the world would that boy quit for, Tom?"

"He said he didn't like no part of it so he was a comin' home to stay. He said a place would be open and I could try for it again!"

Uncle Cummins put his arm around Tom's shoulder and said, "This time I'm going to help you more! I'll go to see some of my friends and ask them for letters of recommendation for you. I've worked hard for this state and a lot of people still owe me a favor or two.''

"Uncle, I need all of the support I can muster to get this appointment. I want to go there. Both of us know I need the education if I ever plan to get a good job. I need a career and the Army would be a good one.''

"You'd make a fine soldier, Tom. I'd be proud to see you in uniform.''

"Yes, Sir, and I'm a'going to Washington to see Congressman Hays about the appointment. Will you go with me? I shore need you.''

"Yes, I'll go. I have a lot of friends in Washington. We'll get up early tomorrow and start out. Go tell Aunt Mary to get our clothes packed; I'll go down to the barn and tell our driver to get the horses and buggy ready. We'd better take our strongest horses on this trip. It will take us a few days to get there.''

With those words, Cummins left to put his plans in action. Tom went to the house to give the message to Aunt Mary. He was excited over the prospect of going to Washington to obtain entry papers for West Point.

Nephew and Uncle were packed and ready to go at the first hint of daylight. It was a beautiful summer morning and as they made their way toward Washington, they talked of the days to come. Along the road they stopped to eat their noonday meal from the basket of food Aunt Mary had packed. Tom took the horses down to the creek to water, and after a few hours rest, they made their way to a little hotel Cummins knew about, arriving a little before dusk.

This was a trip to remember for Tom who had never been out of Virginia, with the exception of a little travel in Kentucky some years before. The stopped at a little hotel and the attendant met them and took the horses to the barn to be watered and fed. Tom and his Uncle entered the hotel for the night.

The accommodations were better than expected. Great soft beds with feather mattresses and soft down pillows. The crisp white sheets felt good to their weary bodies as they blew out the lamp and settled down for the night. It was hard for them to get to sleep. They had enjoyed going into the large dining room at the hotel for supper as the food was delicious and both of them had eaten too much. Tom sighed and turned over as the soft breeze and the song of the night bird lulled him to sleep.

The rest of the trip was interesting but uneventful. Uncle Cummins was familiar with the territory so he spent some time talking about various landmarks along the way. Finally they could see Washington as they rounded a bend in the road and made their way down the cobblestone streets toward the inn. It was dusk and they could see lamps burning in the windows of the beautiful brick homes. Tom was interested in the lamplighter who was walking along the road, stopping to light the oil lamps on the tall poles.

They drove up to the inn and told the attendant to keep the horses for about three days, then they went in. The scene was one Tom would never forget. Ladies in their long taffeta dresses with bonnets to match and gentlemen dressed in frock coats with starched shirts, each carrying a gold headed cane. This was a mode of dress completely unfamiliar to Tom. His experience with dress was narrowed to work clothes of homespun material. He knew nothing of city life.

The inn was ablaze with light and as they entered, an attendant came up and took their bags. Cummins signed a book at the desk and they proceeded up the flight of stairs which led to the bedrooms on the second floor. Tom had never seen such luxury! Plush red carpet on the floor and damask drapes with lace curtains at the windows. The furniture was of the finest wood and polished to gleaming beauty. The tables held hand painted lamps which, when lighted by the attendant, gave a soft glow to the room.

Young Tom looked around and wondered if he would ever be rich enough to afford such furniture in a home of his own. Cummins tried to put him at ease. "I'm glad you like it, Nephew. Some day you may have just such a room as this one. You have a wonderful future ahead and if you work hard you'll be somebody!"

"Oh, Uncle, if I can just get this appointment, I'll make you proud of me. I will succeed! I'm gonna make a good soldier."

Cummins took Tom down the hall to a room at the end. He opened the door and for the first time in his life, Tom saw a bathroom, complete with a round tub full of steaming water which the attendant had heated and poured for him.

"It's been a long and dusty ride, Tom. I want you to take a nice hot bath and dress yourself in clean clothes. Then I'll do the same. When we finish, we'll go downstairs and have supper."

"Thank you, Uncle, I shore need a bath," he said as he went back to get his bag and return to the bathroom.

They dressed in their best and went downstairs to the dining room. The place was full of people who were dining on the finest of food. Great tables of steaming platters piled high were set, just ready for the patrons. Serving girls filled their plates on trays and escorted them to a table which was set with crystal and silver.

Uncle and Nephew began to relax as they enjoyed the food and listened to the music. A beautiful lady was playing a harpsichord. Young Tom had never heard such music before.

Rising early the next morning, both men breakfasted on a fine meal and then proceeded to meet with Congressman Hays at his office in the Capitol where Tom presented himself with an air of assurance. The Congressman greeted them and listened to their plea for an appointment to West Point.

Hays was impressed with Tom. True, his scholastic record was not of the highest rank and his appearance was that of a young and awkward young man. But the set of his jaws and lips, with a dead serious look in his blue piercing eyes, made him realize this lad burned with an intensity to achieve his goal, no matter what stumbling blocks were in the way! So he sent him to the War Office for an interview with the Secretary. With this accomplished, they went back to the hotel to wait until the next day when they were to return for an answer.

The next morning, they went back to meet John Tyler, Jr., private secretary to his father, President John Tyler. He had brought from the War Department, the Cadet appointment papers for Thomas Jackson to be signed by the President, as one of his appointments at large. Consequently, Jackson was advised by the War Department that he would be allowed to proceed to West Point where he would have to take the entrance examinations and pass them before admission to the Academy.

Cummins and Tom were ecstatic! At last Tom would have the chance to fulfill his dream. They went back to the hotel and made arrangements for Tom to leave on the next stage for New York. His Uncle spent the rest of the day preparing him for the trip. Cummins bid him goodbye the next morning, then turned and headed back home.

Chapter 3

Thomas Jackson reported to West Point June 20, 1842. His first view of the Point, nestled on a high hill overlooking the Hudson River, was a sight he was never to forget. He walked along the brick path which led to the many buildings, stopping from time to time to inquire the way to the Adjutant's office. His heart pounded as he walked over the threshold and up to a desk where he signed his name in the "Descriptive List of New Cadets for the Year."

One of the cadets, assigned the task of assisting the new plebes, took him to temporary quarters where he would live until he qualified for admission.

The Cadet Candidates were examined for admission on June 23, 24, and 25. The long examination exhausted Tom and by the time he had completed the last page, he felt mentally drained. He welcomed the chance to return to his quarters and wait for the results of the exam. The candidates knew that the names of those who qualified for admission, would be posted on Saturday at 3:00 p.m. Tom went out and waited for the cadet to post the names.

One by one, the candidates passed by the billboard and read the names. Tom stood in line until his turn came and then saw that his name was on the list. It was last but at least it was there! He was admitted to the Academy on July 1, 1842.

Jackson was disappointed with his introduction to the first few months of higher learning at West Point. He thought he would begin with his studies right away. Instead he was sent, along with the other plebes, to a summer encampment until the end of August. It was there he learned the rudiments of drill and discipline.

The plebes lived in flimsy tents and endured temperature extremes of heat, rain and the discomfort of sleeping on bare earth. There was no time for anything except learning the harsh discipline of the Point. He was disgusted and homesick and could understand why Gibson Butcher was dissatisfied and had returned home. He would lie down at night and fight with his conscience. He longed for home and the peaceful, secure life he left but his determination to succeed would always win and he vowed to continue his pursuit of an education and a career.

Jackson worked hard to raise his standing. For an eighteen year old who had reported in homespun clothes, his resolute will to succeed was the only thing that kept him going. He didn't socialize any during the four years he attended the academy. He was so intent on graduating, he studied into the wee hours of the morning by the glow of the fireplace. Fellow cadets respected him for his honesty and perseverance. Dabney Maury once remarked to another cadet, "That fellow looks as if he's come here to stay."

Tom always spoke in a soft, polite voice and he spoke very little. The cadets soon learned that he was not to be toyed with and would not stand for any joking around so they let him alone. He could be seen struggling with his courses, never missing a class or marching drill and always doing his best no matter what was imposed on him.

He wrote often to his sister Laura. He loved her deeply and in his letters he poured out his heart. He told her of his hopes and dreams as well as the disappointments and failures. She always encouraged him and this seemed to mean a lot to Tom. This devotion between them lasted all of their lives.

Jackson's record soon became widely acclaimed by his classmates and the officers. No one thought he would last through four years, but he marshaled his talents and engaged in a war with academics, winning top quarter standings in third class year Mathematics; second class year in Philosophy; and first class year in Ethics, Artillery, Mineralogy, Geology and Engineering. His standing in Conduct, over the four year period, was excellent. During his second class year, he received no demerits and was rated number one in the United States Corps of Cadets in Conduct for 1843-1844.

Jackson had come to the Point as a tall, lean and awkward boy, but the rigorous training and drilling had developed his frame and strengthened his posture. He now had the appearance of a soldier. He had set down a list of rules by which he lived. They related to morals, choice of friends, manners and aims of life. Another contained his favorite maxims with "You may be whatever you resolve to be" heading the list.

It was easy for me to see, in later years, just how Jackson had developed his life. I read his list which included: "Through life let your principal object be the discharge of duty. Disregard public opinion when it interferes with your duty; endeavor to be at peace with all men; sacrifice your life rather than your word and do well everything you undertake." He believed in temperance, silence, frugality, sincerity, justice and moderation. He was intolerant of uncleanliness and waste. His choice of friends was an important selection guided by the maxims; "A man is known by the company he keeps" and "Seek those who are intelligent and virtuous." He did not believe he should have many intimate friends therefore he chose few but did have many acquaintances.

Many of Jackson's classmates told me about his health habits. They soon realized that he was a sensitive person who took his training seriously. This sometimes affected his health to a point that he suffered with dyspepsia. They said he did not believe he should study by leaning over a desk so he sat perfectly straight in his chair, believing that this position would benefit his malady. As the pressures mounted, they could see Jackson frown with discomfort although he never complained about his condition.

Militarily, Cadet Jackson served as a Sergeant in Company "D" United States Corps of Cadets. By the fourth year he had raised his academic standing from one of an average student to a place in the top third of his class. More remarkable was the constancy of the struggle he waged against academics. His record at the Academy mirrors the fighting character, devotion to duty and the will to succeed of the man. He was beginning to develop the traits of a genius and as we learned, many years later, this same man would also be fighting in the crucial years of the Civil War with or against some of his clasmates such as, Hamilton, Woods, Hazzard, McAllister, Van Buren, Chalfin, Wilcox, Mason, Dickerson, Tillinghast, Fry, Gibson, Burnside, Gibbon, Ayres, Heth, Griffin, Hendershott, Moore, Neill, Bums, Hunt, Blake, Couch, Foster, Gibbons, A. P. Hill, D. R. Jones, McClellan, Maury, Picket, Reno, W. D. Smith, and Stoneman.

Graduation day, July 1, 1846, arrived. Waking early, he went to the window to look out upon the scene which would become indelible in his memory. He stared at the grounds where he would soon go to receive his diploma. This was the day he had so long awaited and was thankful that

Uncle Cummins and Laura had written to tell him that they would be there for his graduation.

Tom dressed carefully for the ceremony. Resplendent in his uniform, with brass polished to perfection and boots gleaming, he made his way down the stairs to join his classmates. He could look through the glass in the hall and see a crowd of people gathering. They filed slowly toward the chairs which had been set up in front of the podium. These were the peole who meant most to the men...family, friends and sweethearts—all waiting to see them receive that coveted parchment which represented four years of hard work.

The band began to play the processional march and the men filed out to take their places. They listened to the General welcome the visitors and to his message directed toward the graduates. Tom listened to every word, absorbing each meaning so he could remember it forever. He could still not believe that he had actually made the grade.

Then the great moment came! Each man's name was called and as he reached the podium he was handed the diploma and given a hand shake. Finally, the last man received his and a great cheer went up from the throng. Tom Jackson was no longer that awkward boy in homespun clothes who shyly knocked on the door of the Adjutant's office. He was Lieutenant Jackson, a graduate of West Point!

Laura and Uncle Cummins had been watching the ceremony but Tom had not seen them. They hurried over to where he was standing and with outstretched arms, gathered him to them. Laura kissed him and Uncle Cummins grasped his hand.

"Tom, we are so proud of you! You look wonderful in your uniform and nothing like the young man who left Lewis County " Laura said as she put her hand on his shoulder and rubbed the smooth uniform. She was so glad to see Tom in some decent clothes.

Uncle Cummins reached in his breast pocket and pulled out an envelope.

"Here son, this is for you. I've been waiting for this day a mighty long time. You have made me proud and I call you son because you are the son I never had. The good Lord blessed me when you came to live with us!"

Tom took the envelope and opened it. It was a bank draft for more money than he had ever seen!

"Uncle Cummins, I don't deserve such a present as this. You are too good to me...but thank you sir, I'll use it wisely!"

"I want you to have a nest egg. You need money to spend on your leave and enough to get started at whatever you plan to do."

They were walking back toward Tom's quarters by then. He stopped at the door and said, "You two come in and wait in the visitors' area while I go up and get my bags. I have everything packed and ready to go."

"Yes," Laura said, "get your things and go back to the hotel with us. We have already planned a celebration and have a room reserved for you."

They went to the hotel, where Tom had his bags taken to his reserved space and then met Laura and Uncle Cummins in the lobby. They went into the dining room for dinner. The room was full of graduates and their families celebrating in the same manner. A gala atmosphere pervaded the hotel as exchanges of congratulations and good wishes took place.

There were toasts coming from people all over the room and the spirit of comraderie continued as the men greeted each other walking from table to table to be introduced to friends. It was a time when they felt restrictions could be cast aside for a day of celebration.

"What are your plans, Tom?" Cummins asked.

"Well, sir, I want to visit Laura and her family for a while and then I want to return to our home in Jackson Mills and stay with you until I decide what is best. We need to talk over my plans."

Laura clasped her hands in excitement, "Brother, you have just made me so happy. You haven't met Will and you have never seen the children. We were hoping you would want to spend some time with us."

Laura had married shortly after Tom entered West Point. He couldn't get a leave to go the wedding. They had moved to Beverly, Virginia.

"Tom, that will be a good plan. You go back with Laura and I'll return to Jackson Mills tomorrow. This will give me time to prepare for your visit."

Tom left them that night to have a final few hours with some of the graduates who were staying in the hotel. He sat with them and listened to their thoughts of the past four years. Each had a plan for the future and many of them wanted to go to Mexico. Tom told them he had applied for an appointment and was looking for his papers to be sent to his Uncle's address.

The day had been long and exciting. All of the men were given furloughs and were planning to leave the next morning for their respective homes. They shook hands, said their final goodbyes and retired to their rooms.

The next morning, Tom and Laura took a stage back to Beverly. The two day trip was broken by a night spent at a little hotel on the side of the mountain. They had time for a long walk that afternoon. It brought back memories of their childhood when the two of them used to explore trails

THOMAS J. JACKSON,

and imagine they were going into some enchanted forest. They laughed and talked as they made their way along the trail, finally walking back to the hotel for supper.

The peace and quiet of that little place was a far cry from his noisy existence of the past four years, where every move was dictated by the sound of bells and bugles coupled with the marching feet of his classmates. He and Laura enjoyed a nice, leisurely dinner, catching up on the activities of the past four years. It was a good feeling to be with his sister whom he adored, with money in his pocket and a military future assured. He looked forward to his career in the Army.

The next day's journey was not complicated by bad weather or trouble. They arrived in Beverly in early afternoon and Will met them. He walked up to Tom and said, "Welcome, Tom. I'm so glad you decided to visit us. I've been looking forward to meeting you for almost four years."

"Thank you, Will. It's nice to be back among my family again. Where are the children?"

"I left them with their nurse. Nancy and Will, Jr. are still taking naps. By the time we get there, they will be up and full of energy. We spent many hours explaining to them that their Uncle was coming so they are very excited!"

Laura and Will's home was beautiful. Tom could see that Laura had made a good choice when she married him. He was a good business man and provided well for her and the children. They had servants who met them at the driveway. "Uncle" John, a combination butler and driver, took their bags up to the bedrooms. He helped Tom then went downstairs to see that the cook knew the family would want an afternoon tea.

Tom unpacked, then went downstairs to the veranda where Laura and Will were sitting. Little Nancy and Will, Jr. were there and waiting to be introduced to their uncle.

He looked at the children then walked over to pick them up. It was like seeing his mother's face again as he looked at Nancy. She had the same coloring, hair and eyes that had been familiar to him as a child. Will, Jr. looked like his father and was the first to speak.

"Uncle Tom we've been waiting so long to see you. Tell us about the Army. Papa says you are going to march and live with the soldiers."

"Yes Will, someday soon, I'll be with the soldiers, but for right now, I'm going to enjoy a visit with you."

Nancy shyly put her arms around his neck and cuddled close. She was just two but she seemed to know that he was family. Tom had missed the closeness he felt with his loved ones.

The maid brought tea, a tray of sandwiches, and little cakes. The children were delighted having a "tea party" with the grown ups. Tom looked around at the surrounding countryside and the shady porch which was furnished with tables and rockers. It was just like a summer living room. "What a perfect setting for Laura" he thought. She had always been the perfectionist in the family and now she and Will had a home which reflected her loving personality. He felt good about her and would not worry when he had to leave again.

The next few lazy days were spent visiting the countryside, going to Will's store and meeting their friends. Laura and Will were well established in the community. She worked with the church and Will had various civic duties. The children were going to be brought up in a nice community and this mattered to Tom for he and Laura had been pushed from one relative to another until Uncle Cummins took them.

A few days later, he bid his sister and the family goodbye and went to visit Uncle Cummins. He got off the stage in Charlottesville where Uncle Cummins was waiting for him. They took the familiar road back and Lieutenant Jackson knew he was going home. After all, this was the only real "home" he had ever known!

They passed the creek, going over the bridge toward the farm. The old barn and the stables where his uncle kept the race horses, had changed little. And when they drove up to the old home Tom was surprised to see that a new roof was on it, the shutters painted and the windows gleamed as if they had just been washed. He knew that someone had been working hard.

"It looks like you folks have been doing a might of work around here, Uncle Cummins. Sure does look nice!"

"Well, I tell you, boy. When the slaves found out you were coming home they were so tickled they most worked themselves to death. Aunt Mary brought in every girl she could to help her get ready for your visit. The cook has put up your favorite preserves and pickles and she had these men working day and night to bring in the meat for your dinner. They had to get the finest ham out of the smokehouse, then she cooked up a pot of your favorite chicken and dumplins' and that's not all. She has a whole sideboard lined with cakes and pies. I hope you're hungry 'cause she means to fill you up."

Aunt Mary came running out of the house and down the steps to greet Tom. She was so happy the tears were rolling down her cheeks. Now and then she would take the corner of her white apron and wipe the tears away.

"Lawsy, mas Tom, I sho' glad to see you. Turn around and let me see how fine you look in that uniform."

Tom grabbed Aunt Mary and hugged her, "Aunt Mary, I'm sure glad to get home to you and folks. 'I need some of that good home coooking, but most of all I need your mothering. It's been a long time since I had anyone to do something for me.''.

Tom went up the steps to his room. He was pleased to see that everything was just as he left it, even to the clothes in the wardrobe. His old fishing hat was hanging on the same hook and his boots were put neatly on the floor. The crisp white curtains swayed gently in the summer breeze and the white counterpane on the bed was just as he remembered it. He looked at the fireplace and recalled how many hours he had studied by the flame. The wash basin and pitcher painted with blue and pink roses, looked as if it had not been moved off the table since he left. The soap dish, with his favorite soap, his towel folded neatly on the rack beside the wash stand were the familiar things he had missed for four years. It was good to be home!

The lieutenant enjoyed the visit with the folks at Uncle Cummins' farm, chatting with friends and traveling the familiar paths which led to the first school and church he attended. When he walked up the little wooden steps leading into the Church, he had a deep feeling of being close to his Lord. Although he had been attending religious service regularly while at West Point, the feeling was not that of the closeness he felt in the Church of his childhood. He walked into the sanctuary and down the aisle to the seat where he had always sat with Laura and Uncle Cummins. There he stopped, knelt down and offered a prayer of thanksgiving that his Lord had let him get through the last four years. He knew that he faced an unfamiliar life and asked for Divine protection as he ventured out into a world which was unknown to him. He felt very grateful that he had been allowed such an opportunity and gave the Lord credit for his success. He asked for guidance and as he finished his prayer and turned around, he saw the minister standing in the back of the church.

"Tom Jackson, I might have known I would meet you here. I'm proud that you would come to your Church and pray. Makes me think that your early days had meaning."

"Yes sir, Reverend, this place means a lot to me. You don't know how often I thought about it during these last four years! In fact, sometimes when things were bad, the only thing that kept me going was the memory of my Lord, this Church and the friends I had here."

They talked a few minutes about his plans for the future when Tom bade him goodbye and made his way back home. The sun was going down over the horizon as he walked across the bridge. He stopped to admire the still, cool water in the creek, remembering the days when he swam and fished there. Ah, what wonderful soothing memories!

The Colonel of the militia in Weston paid uncle Cummins and Tom a visit, shortly after Tom arrived. He wanted to talk with them about the muster parade he had planned.

"Tom, you are the town's returning West Point graduate. We don't have another one around and we are proud of you. It's not often we have the honor of showing off someone like you!"

"Thank you, sir. It's good to be back among my friends. Four years is too long to be away from home."

"Now, getting back to the subject, Tom. We want you to take command of a company for the muster parade."

Tom thought for a minute, then with a slight tinge of military professionalism, he replied, "No, sir. I don't think that would be proper because I probably wouldn't understand your orders. I haven't marched with the men and they wouldn't understand my commands!"

"Come now, Tom. We'd be mighty disappointed if you turned us down," replied the Colonel looking upset over his answer.

"Well, sir, I can try it but I don't know how it will work out. I hate to disappoint you though."

"Then it's settled. I insist. Meet me at the parade grounds tomorrow at 10 a.m.."

The Colonel, his mission accomplished, got up to leave. "Cummins, you should be mighty proud of this boy. You've done a good job of raising him."

"Thank you, Colonel. We'll see you tomorrow morning."

Jackson and his uncle went out to the parade grounds early the next day. The Colonel met them and escorted Jackson to the company he was to command. Jackson saw that they were a group of elderly and untrained volunteers who obviously know little about the fine elements of a military parade. His heart sank as he listened to the Colonel explain to the men that he would be leading them. It was too late now, he'd have to do the best he could.

The signal was given, drums rolled and the men assembled. The Colonel mumbled an order, which Jackson did not understand. Jackson took his place and issued his first command, "March!"

The men marched forward, then Jackson wanted them to return. "To the rear, march!"

The old volunteers paid no attention to the command and proceeded to march right on to the edge of the field. Jackson yelled again, "To the rear, march!"

The men kept on going and to his horror, they proceeded off the field and down toward the only street in town.

"Halt!"

No response, the men kept on marching as Jackson frantically tried to get their attention. He could see they were approaching the railroad tracks, and he could hear the train coming. He knew he must stop them or they would keep right on going.

There was an open field by the side of the tracks. Jackson ran to the front of the column, held up his hands and yelled, "Left turn!"

Pointing in the direction of the field, he managed to make his command heard and the men made a left turn.

"Left flank," he yelled as he stayed in front of them until he could turn around and give another command. "Left turn!"

Now he had them back on the road leading to the parade grounds. "March," he said and they followed Jackson back to the grounds where be brought them up in front of the astonished crowd.

"Halt!" The men stopped in front of the Colonel who was livid with frustration and anger.

"Salute to the colors!" The men saluted.

"Company dismissed!"

The Colonel walked up to Tom asking, "Tom, why did you take the men through town?"

"Sir, those were your orders. That was your command and I followed it." Only then did the Colonel realize what he had done and sheepishly apologized for the mistake.

Tom's friends were impressed by his actions and many of them were inspired to join the militia. They had never seen such regimentation but they liked it and wanted to become a part of the Army.

Two days later, Tom received his orders. He was to proceed to Fort Columbus, Governor's Island, New York and report to Capt. Francis A. Taylor, commanding K Company, First Artillery. On July 23, Jackson said goodbye to Uncle Cummins and left for New York.

Chapter 4

Lieutanent Jackson reported to Fort Columbus and found that Captain Taylor had left for Fort Hamilton, New York. He showed the officer his papers and was immediately sent to Fort Hamilton to join Captain Taylor.

Fort Hamilton was a large and busy post. It took Jackson quite a while to find Captain Taylor.

"Sir, I am Lieutenant Thomas Jackson, here to report to you."

"Good, Lieutenant. I've been expecting you. We have been alerted for a move to Mexico. I'll have one of the men show you to your quarters. Get your gear ready and we will be moving out tomorrow!"

Taylor called for Jackson late that evening.

"I need to discuss this movement of troops with you, Lieutenant. We will leave at dawn and take thirty men, forty horses and our equipment on a march which will eventually lead us to Pittsburgh. From there, we'll take a river boat to New Orleans and on to Point Isabel, Texas. That will be our base of operations. No need to tell you this will be a long, hard march."

"I know, sir. I welcome the chance to serve under your command and I want you to know you can count on me."

"I do know I can count on you. You have come highly recommended. I need the best men I can get to make this trip."

With that, the two men saluted and parted until morning.

The thirty-six days march was long and hard. They stopped often to let the men rest, not wanting to begin their tour with any exhausted or sick troops. It would take a full company to enter into the fierce fighting which lay ahead. The morale was good and it was easy for Jackson to see why. Taylor was ready for a real battle and the men had picked up his enthusiasm!

They reached Pittsburgh, then boarded a river boat and steamed down the Ohio and Mississippi Rivers to New Orleans. Many of the men had not been this far south and had to become accustomed to the humidity and heat of the southern climate. There was tension in the air as the troops, horses and guns prepared for the sea trip to Point Isabel, Texas!

My first recollection of meeting Lieutenant Jackson was on that trip to Point Isabel. I was a Sergeant in Company K., in charge of supplies. He came up to me as we boarded the boat in New Orleans and asked whether I had checked all of our supplies and did I know of anything we needed before we sailed?

"No sir, Lieutenant. I've been real careful to load everything we need for this trip. They tell me there ain't much at Point Isabel. Seems like the Mexicans have burned most everything up there."

The men were loading their equipment on the boat in preparation for an early sailing. Jackson walked around the deck. He and Captain Taylor met in the cabin to check their plans. The wind had picked up and as the two men looked out over the Gulf of Mexico, they noticed the Eastern sky. Ominous clouds had formed and the water was swirling under their boat. Waves rushed toward the shore and as they looked over the stretch of beach, they saw the intensity of the storm which was brewing.

"Looks like we're in for some bad weather, sir. Some of the local people said it looks like we could have a hurricane. Have you ever been in one?"

"No, I haven't, but if they think so, then we'd better get some of them in here to tell us what to do."

Jackson went to the loading dock and asked one of the men to come with him. He took him to Captain Taylor.

"Placide, you've been living here all of your life. Tell us what you can about this storm or hurricane as you people call it."

The Cajun looked at the sky and then at the white capped waves which were now rushing into the shore.

"Mai oui, Cap'n Taylor, indeed we are waiting for da storm. For days the animals and da bugs, dey say to beware. Pelicans and gulls that live on the islands have fly by, goin' to higher ground, they be. The ants have left the mounds. They climbed the trees, high up."

"Dem clouds," said Placide, pointing to the swirling grey mass, "say the wind she gonna blow. A hurricane come for sure, soon. The tide she gonna rise up like a wall, the wind will scream and da trees, they blow away like thistle in da breeze. Bad it gonna be. Dat for sure.''

Captain Taylor looked from the Cajun to his men who were watching the wind begin to whip in the tops of the trees. ''What would you suggest we do?'' asked the Captain.

''You ask me, first you gotta take boat from shore to a long shallow bayou where safe it will be.''

''Do you know of such a place?''

''Sure, where I live is safe. My friends, they will help,'' said Placide.

''Where are your friends, now?''

''They be down by the bayou. I'll send for them now,'' said Placide as he signaled a friend to come. They talked a moment and then Placide's friend left to get help.

''After de boat secured tight, better if your men go to the Army post til the storms blows over.''

Captain Taylor and Jackson thanked him as he left the boat to issue orders to those who were helping to load the ship. Then the Captain and Lieutenant sprang into action, barking out orders, rushing the men to stow the materials as quickly as possible.

As soon as the supplies were loaded and lashed down securely, Placide again boarded the boat to direct them to the bayou and safe harbor. Shortly after getting under way Placide pointed to an opening in the trees. ''We go there!''

Captain Taylor looked at the small opening doubtfully, but issued the order to the helmsman.

As the ship approached the mouth of the bayou, the men along the deck could see the current running in what appeared to be a narrow channel. Keeping to the center there was enough water to accommodate the shallow draft boat. Progressing, they rounded a bend while overhanging limbs grabbed at the men. Cyprus knees stuck out of the water along the banks where the black water stood. Captain Taylor had never seen such a place and was fascinated. The wind raged overhead in the tall pines. The sky was partially blocked by the foliage crisscrossing the bayou. Large vines, as thick as a man's arm grew among the trees, choking the trunks into grotesque shapes. Clusters of lavender flowers hung from the vines. The sweet smell of the wisteria merged with the stale odor of the stagnant water where the incessasnt mosquito bred.

Further along the bayou some of Placide's friends were waiting. They moved along the water until the boat shuddered to a loud halt; the banks on each side closed in on the vessel.

Stout ropes were fastened to the boat, run across the decks and the cargo, to be secured to the massive trees far into the undergrowth.

"Why don't you tie them to the trees right here?" asked the Captain.

Shaking his head, Placide explained, as much with hand gestures as with words, "The water, she rise, bayou get wide, deep. Dem trees, their roots in de water, will be gone with de tide. Have to tie to trees with deep roots in de ground."

The men worked quickly, with one eye constantly on the rising wind and water.

"How are we doing on time?" Captain Taylor asked Placide.

"Comme ci, comme ca," replied Placide.

Finishing the job, Placide and his friends led the Captain and his men down a path inland, toward headquarters and safety.

Captain Taylor stopped a few yards up the path and looked back at the ship and supplies and wondered if they would still be there when the hurricane was over.

The full force of the wind hit the men when they left the shelter of the woods to cross the clearing near headquarters.

"Poo-yie!" cried one of the Cajuns as he leaned into the wind to regain his balance. All the men did the same and hurried toward the barracks as the heavy rain began to sting their faces and arms.

I can tell you right now, that I, Caleb Joshua Sparks, had a lot of respect for the approaching storms. I had heard about them from some of my relatives who visited us.

The men of Company K lay down on their blankets in the barracks, listening to the screeching wind and cracking trees. They could hear the tall pines as they bent to the ground with the force of the wind, and snapped. The grating sound above was the roof of the barracks as it tore and splintered. The most terrifying sound came from the tornadoes spawned from the storm. Bits of debris hit the building and at one time, the door flew open, letting the rain pour in. Some of the men went out and secured it, but wasted not a minute in returning to shelter.

I thought to myself, this is war…just a different kind! All of us wondered if anything would be left of our supplies come daylight!

About three that morning, there was a dead calm. The men relaxed and began to prepare for going out to see what damage the storm had wrought. Placide had stayed with us and when he saw the men preparing to go outside, stopped them, "No, no, bon ami! The storm, she is not over. The quiet, it is the eye. Soon she come again, stronger. From the other direction de wind will come. For sure it will come."

He was right, for the storm came back and this time it nearly flattened our barracks. By daylight, it had calmed down and we were able to go out.

Captain Taylor and Jackson made the first move. They opened the door, pushing debris aside so we could follow. If I had not known what had happened, I would have sworn we'd been in a battle. Buildings were crushed, trees were down everywhere, the pier was gone and the loading dock was floating close to where the ship would have been.

Taylor and Jackson assessed the damage and determined that the first thing we needed to do was repair the loading dock and pier. Jackson called to the men and delegated jobs to them. Placide had his men working and through their assistance, we soon had the pier back in place and a loading dock attached.

With the dock finished it was time to see if we still had a ship. Rather than struggle through the woods Placide and his friends took us to the bayou by pirogue, a canoe-type boat made from a cypress log. The bayou we had sailed the ship into the day before was now wider where trees overhanging the banks had been ripped away. The remaining trees were swept bare of leaves, the branches gnarled and bent. Paddling around the final bend Captain Taylor and the men were elated to see their ship, still intact and the majority of the cargo still on board. Some of the ropes that had secured the ship had torn away and were tangled among the trees along the bank. Spanish moss lay in clumps on deck where the wind had tossed it in its fury.

Thanks to the knowledge of the Cajuns, our ship was safe and we would be able to complete our trip as planned and only a day or two behind schedule.

Getting the ship out of the bayou was not as easy as getting it there had been, but all the men worked together and in a few hours the boat was docked safe and sound at the newly repaired pier.

We set up a mess tent and fed the hungry men. It was getting too late to start so we had to spend another night in the barracks. That night was much quieter than the one before. We were introduced to a card game called bouree, relaxed, and regained our strength for the journey ahead.

Surviving the hurricane was an experience we would never forget. We were all mighty happy to be alive!

The morning dawned clear and bright. The only trace we had of the storm was the floating debris and driftwood. We sailed out of the harbor and headed toward Texas. There were no incidents on that trip. We arrived on September 24th in Point Isabel.

We found out that Monterey had been captured but with this good news we learned that a cessation of hostilities for eight weeks was mutually agreed

OF THE TREES 55

to by the United States and Mexico. It appeared that there would be no chance for any action for some time. We were disappointed as there was very little to do in Point Isabel. Our army converted the town into an immense warehouse for supplies and stores. There was plenty of activity but it was all non-combat army business.

It did not take long for Jackson to tire of garrison duty. Most of his time was spent installing guns in the Point Isabel defenses and he had been assigned as the acting assistant commisary of the company. Not very long after Jackson was stationed at Point Isabel, he met Lt. Daniel Harvey Hill, a fellow West Pointer of the class of 1842. This chance encounter was one of many that Lieutenant Jackson would recall in years to come when the fate of the nation hung in the balance during the critical years of the Civil War.

Despite the armistice, President Polk and the War Cabinet decided to initiate a resumption of the war in order to influence the Mexican Congress which was about to begin deliberations in early December. The existing armistice was terminated and Saltillo was to be occupied. The High Command had good reason for wanting to take over the state of Coahuila as it guarded the strategic pass through the Sierra Madre mountains and overlooked a rich and plentiful granary from which the army could muster supplies. Saltillo would be an excellent military support for Monterey.

General William J. Worth and his group were ordered to take the city. The troops were delighted to get into action again and happy for the decision to a change of scene. When the Americans arrived in Saltillo, the Mexicans had deserted the area leaving only the civilians. The Americans knew that they were in hostile country and that the local population would not permit them to rest on their laurels. Jackson became part of the occupation force in this little agricultural town and had no choice except to wait for developments.

When the Mexican Congress met in December, they elected a president dedicated to resistance, General Antonio Lopez de Santa Anna. He would seriously complicate American plans. America had to develop a new strategy, and it was decided to land an amphibious expedition somewhere on the eastern coast of Mexico and proceed inland.

Just a month prior to Santa Anna's election, President Polk had decided to put the combined Army-Navy attack expedition under the command of General Winfield Scott. He was the most qualified for the assignment although his politics were controversial and at odds with the administration.

Scott had waited a long time for this plan wanting to lead an amphibious attack against Vera Cruz and capture that fortress city. He could then direct us to the National Road as an invasion route to Mexico City. A number of

Scott's regular troops were to come from Taylor's Army. Worth's division joined Scott and with it went the First Artillery. Jackson got his wish for he moved his company from Saltillo to Camp Palo Alto, Texas and back to Point Isabel, all preparatory for General Scott's plan.

The combined invasion attempt was to be made by the United States Army beginning at Point Isabel as a port of embarkation. There would be more than 15,000 men, horses, mules, cannons, wagons, ambulances, ammunition, blankets and supplies to be shipped. This in itself caused the first logistical snarl because of the scarcity of shipping. General Worth's cavalry and artillery, General David E. Twiggs' troops and General Robert Patterson's fighting men from Tampico were either stranded or delayed. It took quite a period of time to assemble, mobilize and deploy such an expeditionary force. For Lieutenant Jackson, it had been a long and frustrating wait. He knew Scott was going to fight and that is what he wanted to do. He hated to leave Taylor but the excitement of actual combat and the anticipation of being involved in fighting the War was more important to him.

Jackson looked out over the scene and observed the efficiency of the entire operation. The small transport that would carry his men seemed insignificant in the armada. The ships were jammed together with thousands of excited soldiers ready and waiting to go ashore and attack.

Scott decided that they would reach land at a site on the beach opposite the island of Sacrificios approximately some two and a half miles from the city and far from the Mexican guns. The troops were brought in to the beaches in amphibious waves, with boat after boat landing in selected locations. Jackson and his men, eager for direct attack on the enemy beach heads, followed in the third wave of the assault group. As the troops landed on the beaches a vast array of the conglomerate force used by the Americans could be seen spread out in a panorama of military power and might. The action was sporadic as the American firepower increased while Mexican counterfire and cannonades boomed from the various gun emplacements.

At this point, Jackson experienced strange feelings as he set foot on Mexican soil in actual warfare. He had never fought on foreign shores or participated in any real military engagement, yet he had trained at West Point four years and endured the sacrifices of nights and days of hard work and study to be prepared for the battles he would endure with the coming of hostilities with any foe. He was imbued with the military spirit and youthful ambition to participate and be all victorious in what he considered an invigorating exercise of battle.

The enemy resistance was of a dissonant nature and the American troops swept through it as a scythe through a ripe wheat field. The siege of Vera

Cruz began immediately. Santa Anna's men resisted bravely even though they had not received any reinforcements. The fight dragged on until March 27th when the Mexicans decided to avoid further losses and surrender to the superior fighting power of the American troops. Lieutenant Jackson had a real smell and taste of war during the siege, giving his artillery assistance to General Twiggs and General Worth. He narrowly escaped injury when a cannon ball came within a short distance of him, blowing up part of a battery and killing several horses. He later wrote to Laura to tell her about the battle but the important bit of news was the performance of his troops and the bravery of the American joint command.

Tom revealed a little about himself as he wrote to Laura. She was his confidant and rarely did he discuss similar matters with anyone else. He had little patience with what he called army politics, and often referred to incidents, commenting that he should have been commended for various acts but never received even a mention on paper because of his lower rank. He told Laura that "rank was the only requisite for fame" and that he had not reached that pinnacle yet. Here was Jackson, opening his heart and mind for his dear sister, yet he cautioned her to use discretion in repeating anything he told or wrote her, for it was of utmost importance that news be kept under the blanket of military security. Jackson was the same as all other men who felt that achievement merited recognition but he would not publicly or privately give voice to his feelings hoping that in due time his higherups in the army command would recognize him for whatever deeds he accomplished.

General Scott was anxious to move against Mexico City. His two reasons were that he wanted to take the capital quickly at a minimum cost of men and war material and to avoid the disease of yellow fever. He knew it was the time of year when the "Vomito" or yellow fever was due in this area and he had to get his troops to higher ground. It was in the lowlands that the fever started and prevailed for months on end. Speed was essential therefore and Mexico City must be taken!

General Scott was certain that the Mexicans, led by Santa Anna would be there to fight for their capital but whatever direction they would arrive from to defend Scott's assault was a questionable matter. The American troops would have to be well and their attitude positive in order for an attack on the city to be made successfully.

The objective was to take Cerro Gordo, thus enabling the troops to obtain access to the National Road. While his men held the positions that were in their hands at the end of the day, Scott determined to attack again on the morning of the eighteenth. General Twiggs moved part of his troops far to the right to strike at the National Road close by or above the main Mexican army camp. The rest of the troops on Atalaya were positioned to charge the top of Cerro Gordo.

At about seven o'clock the men on Atalaya struck fiercely and shortly won the Cerro Gordo ground. The Mexican retreat began. When Scott saw the enemy retreating, he began pursuit and pushed hard against the fleeing Mexicans. Not until Scott's driving action became a rout did Jackson become involved in the Cerro Gordo salient. Being an astute observer and noting all of Scott's moves, Jackson mentally recorded all of the actions trying to understand why they were made and wondering at the immense success of each. Such lessons in military brilliance were to remain with Jackson for the rest of his life, coming into good play during the crucial battles of the Civil War in which he was to play such an important role.

The road to Jalapa was now open and cleared. A tired but extremely happy American army reached the capital city of the state of Vera Cruz on April 19th. What they found was a literal "Garden of Eden." The entire area was lush, with colorful flowers, luxuriant foliage and varied types of fruit. The surrounding mountains were snow-topped while East of the city one could see the dazzling blue water of the Gulf of Mexico.

Jackson realized that this would be his temporary home for the next couple of weeks. He was not happy about it as he preferred action and the possibility of military operations which might bring him recognition for heroism and bravery in the face of the enemy. The fighting to eventually take Mexico City would go on even though Jackson and others were sidelined for a short while. Jackson's quest for recognition caused him much frustration yet it was appeased somewhat when he received notice of promotion to Second Lieutenant effective March 3, 1847. He had written Laura that he expected promotion from his graduated West Point status of Brevet Second Lieutenant to that of regular Second Lieutenant in the army. At long last, he was on the road to recognition with hopeful ambitions of rising higher as the war progressed.

"This will give me more rank, which is of the greatest importance in the Army."

There followed a transfer to the heavy artillery. This new assignment kept him in the regiment but shifted him from Company K to Company G.

It now looked like Jackson would have the opportunity to get involved in some heavy fighting. This is what he had hoped for, not only to fight but a chance to gain prominence and distinction. But the plans of youth do not always result in goals attained—not even for a man of Jackson's promising ability or burning ambitions to be outstanding on the battlefield. Luck and chance often play decisive roles in determining the roll of the dice. It looked like another setback loomed for Jackson. Just when it seemed he might have a chance to join the advance positions at Perote, the Jalapa military governor, Brevet Colonel Thomas Childs took charge of the First Artillery as part of the garrison group and Jackson was assigned to stay with his company. To say that Jackson was hurt and humiliated would be putting it mildly. The only thing that saved his grace and temporarily assuaged his feelings was his new religion. He wrote to Laura, commenting,

"The only thing I can do is to throw myself into the hands of an all Wise God and hope that it may all be for the better. It may have been one of His means of diminishing my excessive ambition; and after having accomplished His purpose, whatever it may be, He, then, in His Infinite Wisdom may gratify my desire!" Jackson had learned humility and experienced his really first sign of what he later believed to be Preordination!

Taylor and Jackson began talking about religion despite the fact that the Lieutenant had never brought himself around to joining a church. They had often discussed their beliefs and compared thoughts about a God who ruled the world. The young Lieutenant was very curious. The acceptance of his fate was entrenched in his mind. Although he was unaware of it, he was beginning to live part of the faith of the Presbyterian church.

I watched my new friend Tom Jackson, as he spent his idle time in Jalapa. He took up the study of the Spanish language. He had told me that he needed to learn the language so he could better understand the people...but there was another reason...he had serious thoughts of taking up the acquaintance of some lady.

This came as a surprise...yet it should not have. Here was a young man, serious and aspiring to gain recognition in his military career, a perfectionist in every sense of the word, yet just as human as the rest of us. He was strongly feeling the need for female companionship. It made me feel better to know that he had a finer side hidden deep within that cool and military developed conscience.

Jackson roamed about the countryside looking at the exotic plants and tasting the strange fruit. The natural beauty of the place interested him. He learned to like the fruits and would spend some time each day sampling first one kind and then the other. His health had improved, and he had gained some much needed weight.

A new light artillery battery was authorized as a result of a general order by General Scott. The new company to be formed would be Company I, First Regiment, Captain John B. Magruder commanding. Two Lieutenants would be needed to assist Magruder and Jackson resolved to be one of them.

He admired Magruder immensely and knew that the Captain always seemed to know where the fighting was and always personally involved himself in the very thick of the engagement. Jackson applied for the new assignment and got it, hurriedly catching up with his new captain around Puebla but not before engaging the enemy where he was credited with killing four of the Mexicans in combat. This was the first time that he had the experience of drawing blood. It was a first time happening for him and he treated it cooly as a routine matter.

General Scott's troops were stalled in the city awaiting ammunition replenishment, food and reinforcements. Jackson took the time to better acquaint himself with his commanding officer and the men serving with Company I. In due time, he became second in command of Magruder's battery, a position which he relished and which put him in charge of a section of the guns in action. The attraction of the Captain and Lieutenant for each other was mutual and a strong friendship developed.

The war was going well for the Americans. Scott was ready for the campaign against the capital city but problems developed because of a shortage of experienced troops for the initial onslaught.

General Scott knew that many volunteers left as their enlistment period expired and he was reasonably certain that the administration in Washington would not send him any more men. Despite the shortage in manpower, he decided to advance on August 7th and take his chances with the troops that were left. The Cerro Gordo veterans led by General Twiggs took the lead, marching for four days and crossed the mountains at an elevation of 10,000 feet. Their first glimpse of the Valley of Mexico was a scene of thrilling beauty.

The capital of Mexico, the American objective and ultimate goal which would terminate the war lay a half mile down and about twenty miles west. Many pitfalls existed between the army and Mexico City, including three lakes, marshy ground, various arroyos and the ever present guerrillas and bandidos. All of the causeways, bridges and tunnels were strongly fortified and were an integral part of the Mexican defense system. The General sent his engineers out to probe all defenses of the enemy on approaches to the city. One of the most reliable of these engineers was a Captain Robert E. Lee, a brilliant and brave officer who was to play his greatest role in the bloody Civil War of 1861-1865.

On August 14th, General Scott received a report that the road south of Chalco and Xochimilco was passable but difficult because of its very rough and rocky contours. The General decided to flank Santa Anna's eastern defense and to turn the Mexican position by proceeding against the city from the south.

A plan was put into operation in which General Twiggs and his troops were to remain at Ayotla to cause the Mexicans to think that the Americans were going to attack the batteries at El Penon. General Worth supported by Generals Pillow and Quitman were to take the southern road, heading for the small town of San Augustin. By August 17th, the group was some nine miles from Mexico City and on a straight line through the village of Churubusco to the capital itself. Before entering Mexico City there was another problem with which the army had to contend; a huge ancient lava area called the Pedregal which would have to be crossed.

Captain Robert E. Lee was assigned the task. Taking a small escort, he carefully scouted and surveyed the entire lava field to find a way to turn Santa Anna's flank. He found a way on how to do this and on August 19th the army began digging and laying out a road across the Pedregal. Captain Lee had guns brought up including Magruder's light battery and had them moved into position close to the western edge of the field. General Scott knew that the American guns would be outpowered by the Mexicans but they would divert attention while the infantry tried to outflank Santa Anna.

Captain Magruder performed very well. The enemy was bluffed and Jackson got another taste of fiery action as his spirits soared with the noise and sound of the belching cannons. The death of another officer in the battery gave Jackson command of a section of guns employed in the Pedregal in one of Magruder's main positions. Fierce fighting continued for hours as the American forces came under shattering cannon fire which could not be stopped by Magruder and Jackson. The Americans were caught between two enemy forces with a combined number of some 7,000 men plus devastating artillery superiority.

All during the action that followed, Jackson handled himself with outstanding bravery and exceptional skill. His cannon blazed constantly and when Magruder's guns inched forward a little, Jackson came up in dual support waving his arms and shouting orders like a banshee. The troops were sweating and straining to keep the shells loaded into the big guns and the sounds were deafening as cannon after cannon boomed out its fiery load. Captain Magruder could not restrain his enthusiastic admiration for Jackson's behavior and was so pleased that he singled him out in his report to the commanding General, saying "His conduct was equally conspicuous during the whole day and I cannot too highly commend him to the Major General's favorable consideration." Of course Lieutenant Jackson was happy about the commendation!

The Mexican General Valencia incorrectly reasoned that the American troops were in retreat. The rain came down in torrents soaking the men to the bone, but despite the weather the Americans were about to attack once more. Captain Lee volunteered to cross over the Pedregal lava field in the cold wet darkness of the night to advise headquarters that an attack would be made early in the morning before sun up. He would also request that a diversion of some kind be made by General Scott's headquarters command. When Captain Lee accomplished his mission, the General referred to it as "the greatest feat of physical and moral courage performed by any individual, to my knowledge, during the invasion."

General Twiggs thereupon launched a diversionary attack by having a flank assault led by General Smith with Magruder's battery pinning down the Mexican front shortly after daybreak when fighting resumed. Valencia's remaining troops were chased by the Americans with contact made near San Antonio. With the battle going against them, the Mexicans withdrew north-ward around their fortified positions near Churubusco. As the afternoon waned and the attacking American forces close to the fortifications, General Santa Anna gave up his attempt to hold Churubusco. The Mexican situation appeared to be hopeless.

As the fighting gradually ceased, a short truce was agreed upon so that the peace arbiter for the Americans, one Nicholas Trist, might work on a plan for a cessation of all hostilities. During this period of time, Lieutenant Jackson was promoted to the permanent rank of First Lieutenant and to the brevet rank of Captain. He was quite happy with the reasons given as the first lieutenancy was for "gallant and meritorious conduct at the seige of Vera Cruz" while the brevet captaincy was for "gallant and meritorious conduct in the battles of Contreras and Churubusco." Despite the promotions, Jackson wished for some outstanding but heroic performance on his part which would put his name into prominence before his fellow officers and men. His time came sooner than he expected.

The castle of Chapultepec had been since 1833, the site of Mexico's miltiary school. Its location was very strategic as it stood right in the way of the two main gates to the city itself. Some thirteen guns were used by the enemy to defend the castle with approximately one thousand troops plus the cadet corps from the school itself. It was a formidable objective becuse of its natural strength and location. It created an impressive but massive defense to overcome. The American command knew that it would have a most difficult nut to crack but the attack was targeted for the night of September 11th. The signal to attack was duly given and the guns which were brought up under Captain Lee's command started a bombardment which lasted for some time. Scott was in no particular hurry at this hour and the battle was drawn out in a slow and deliberate manner.

Lieutenant Jackson entered the battle on the left side of the attacking forces; his objective to prevent any Mexican reinforcements. An attempt would be made to close off any withdrawals from the castle and the Mexican defenses. The immediate command was made up of the Eleventh and Fourteenth Infantry plus Jackson's section of Magruder's artillery battery. As the action began against Chapultepec on the morning of the fourteenth, Colonel William Trousdale's troops proceeded along the east side of the causeway but took no direct action in the magnificent assault against the castle. Colonel Trousdale's men ran into Santa Anna reinforcements which were sent to the castle, thus setting the stage for Jackson's heroics.

The advance of Trousdale's Eleventh and Fourteenth Infantry against the reinforcements sent by Santa Anna was delayed by enemy infantry and an isolated one-gun stronghold on the castle hill. The enemy poured a heavy withering fire down on the Colonel's troops, enfilading them with volley after volley. To complicate the situation, Colonel Trousdale was wounded and when Jackson saw this, he raced toward him with his two gun battery and searched for a position which would give him command of the area so that he could return fire against the enemy as rapidly as possible.

Bullets were coming in without end; one of his cannons was knocked out while most of the horses were shot dead or chewed up by the one-cannon fire of the enemy's sole battery. Jackson's men were running around like chickens without heads, not knowing what to do or where to run next to avoid the hail of bullets. The situation was truly desperate.

Jackson appeared cool and oblivious to any of the existing dangers. While his men sought refuge from the incessant hail of bullets and shell fire, cowering behind trees, rocks and ditches, Jackson walked up and down in the storm of shot and lead encouraging them to assist him in moving the one remaining gun and resuming firing it as quickly as possible. He seemed to be protected by an invisible shield and his courage in facing up to the potential fact of death, awakened pride and admiration in every one of his surviving troops. He kept yelling at them, "Press on, men, press on. You have nothing to fear. There is no danger. See, I'm not hit."

The men looked at him as if he had lost his senses. I was the only one who stood by him.

"Here, Sergeant Sparks, let's take this gun and fire it."

"Yes, sir," I said as I helped him with the gun and handed him ammunition. It seemed like all hell had broken loose! Jackson moved like a man possessed and his shouting coupled with his smooth loading of the gun bore indicated a fighter in field action second to none. As Jackson put the gun into action once more, General Worth observed what was going on and ordered him to retire to the protection of the infantry. In the middle of all this action, Magruder came up and having had his horse shot out from under him, picked himself up and jumped across the ditch to Jackson's remaining gun. Jackson was so glad to see him that he and Magruder loaded, swabbed and fired round after round on behalf of their brigade. It was a memorable sequence of events not to be forgotten for a long time.

Lieutenant Jackson stood his ground in front of the American army, with his guns and fortitude, getting off shot after shot at the enemy, refusing to back up one inch, thus turning the flow of battle into the favor of the troops led by the General. The news of Jackson's brave and heroic efforts spread like wildfire up and down the entire front of the Americans.

Jackson's fighting for that day was not yet over; he was just getting started. After silencing the Mexican battery he did not stop to do any repairs on his own gun but hitched up to the wagon limbers and proceeded along the road toward the San Cosme gate. He was far ahead of the attacking force of Colonel Trousdale and would have gone it alone if he had not met Lieutenants Daniel Harvey Hill and Barnard E. Bee. There was a group of some forty soldiers under their command and they asked Jackson if they could join him and his cannon as the group made its way down the road. Jackson agreed to join forces with them but Magruder who had ridden up directly behind them was a bit more cautious. It was Magruder's thinking that they should slow down and wait for the rest of the army to catch up with them. Jackson, Hill and Bee convinced Magruder that it would not be wise to wait and as a result he reluctantly conceded.

Hill and Bee supported the force with their additional firepower and the small group moved on for about a half mile or so before they ran into severe difficulty. General Pedro DeAmpudo suddenly faced the small American force with almost 1500 cavalry, charging into them with a furious rush of shot and shell. The surprise almost overcame the Americans as they reeled from the sudden storm of lead and iron being thrown at them.

The moment had come for Jackson and his partners to go on the offensive. Their combined guns opened a wall of fire which ripped large gaps in the enemy's positions. The Mexicans fought bravely, gathered their forces and retaliated against their American foes. All to no avail! Both sides were pretty well exhausted by this time even though the Americans rallied with several more rounds of well directed shots. The time had come however to halt the action and rest while they waited for the rest of the army to catch up with them. Both sides had fought valiantly but the weariness of battle had taken its toll. Jackson had fought himself out but the feeling that came over him was one of achievement and personal pride in the knowledge that he had nobly acquitted himself in the face of bloody warfare and in the presence of his peers. The concluded action was very close to being the last battle between America and Mexico because on September 14th the victorious American army entered Mexico City and the campaign for the capitol of Mexico was over.

The dirty and "dog tired" army organized the occupation of the capital city. General Scott had a bare 6,000 men to police this city of some 200,000 people but he set up rigid and fair regulations for his army, then set to work to make rules for the conduct of civilians. His main problem was the guerrilla activity. Those caught participating were severely punished; only with this rigid policy and discipline was law and order established and city streets made safe.

The time had come to recognize the heroes and among those honored was Lieutenant Jackson. He was given the brevet rank of major and the highest praise by commanding General Scott. His finest hour came from General Scott in a public commendation ceremony. Although he enjoyed the praise, he felt embarrassed by so much attention.

Magruder was quick to praise Jackson, giving him full recognition for his participation in the battle of Chapultepec and the pursuit towards San Cosme. It wasn't until later that Jackson told his friends that his main concern was the battle and not to draw attention to himself, adding that "the hotter the battle got, the more his fighting blood flowed." he had done what he had come to do...to fight and help win the war. This had been his ultimate goal and by faith, persistance and courage, he had made his mark on history!

No seer could have predicted what Jackson's fate in Mexico was destined to be. His deep and abiding belief in his own destiny was enough to sustain him through the many battles in which he fought. The crucible into which he was thrown was a mere stop gap on his way to immortality in the history of America. Only time and a determined but resolute faith in his Maker lay between him and the coming years. Flashes of genius were apparent in Mexico and his character and personality were being developed in a quiet area south of the borders of the United States. He had his star to follow and with the makeup of his individual personality there was no telling how far he would have to go to reach it!

Chapter 5

The life of Tom Jackson began to change from that of a disheveled, war weary soldier, to that of a polished, relaxed officer of the Army, when he was issued quarters in a hacienda owned by Don Miguel De Lacasa. I remember well how his new role began for I was assigned to help him get situated.

We walked into the lovely grounds, surrounded by lush tropical plants and flowers and followed a cobblestone walk to the entrace. The owner met us.

"Good morning, Lieutenant Jackson. I welcome you to my home."

"Thank you, sir," Jackson replied as he walked into the cool foyer of the room.

"My servants will take care of you and your aide. Just follow him. He will show you to your quarters."

The servant took our gear and we followed him through a long hallway which led to our new quarters. We could not help but notice the beautiful tile floor with intricate designs inlaid to create a pattern of Mexican art. The walls were of a strange type of sandstone which we learned later, would keep the house cool in the heat of a Mexican summer and warm when the temperature dropped in the evening. Great wooden doors with long iron locks were at every entrance. Windows were draped with the finest silk and brocade. The bedroom floors were of polished, wide board, with hand hooked rugs scattered around.

The servant placed our gear on a table and asked if he could help us unpack. Jackson politely thanked him and told him we preferred to unpack our things. He showed us the other rooms which consisted of a sitting room and another bedroom for me. A small ante-room was for dressing. It also contained a wash stand and a large marble tub, the likes of which we had never seen before! We thanked him as he prepared to leave. He promised to return with hot water for our bath.

We had never seen such luxury!

Jackson looked at me and said, "Sgt. Sparks, I guess we are going to live well for a while."

"Yes sir, Lieutenant. I'm going to enjoy this soft living after what we've been through!"

We spent the rest of the day unpacking and getting our gear put up. Then we had the luxury of a hot bath and a fresh shave, donning clean uniforms and putting on polished boots which we had allowed the servants to shine.

Don Miguel met us as we walked into the long dining room for supper. He was a gracious host who had opened up his home to the officers and obviously intended to see to their every need. We dined on sumptuous fare that evening. I could see Jackson beginning to relax and eat the strange food. I secretly hoped the hot, spicy food would not give him a return of his dyspepsia. He seemed to be enjoying it so I hoped for the best.

Don Miguel asked what the men would like to do that evening. Since none of them were familiar with the customs, he suggested they attend a musical program with native dances. They agreed that would be very relaxing as they had not had any recreation in months. He ordered the band to arrange a concert and national dancing in the patio area, just off the gardens of the hacienda. The festivities would start at eight-thirty that evening.

Jackson was somewhat hesitant about participating in such an evening. He knew there would be wine and liquor served and after his one and only drinking spree with the men at West Point, he had vowed never to drink again. He decided to attend because he was curious about the native dancing as well as the music.

He wandered over to the patio area as the sun began to set, conversing and making small talk with some of the officers while they waited for the program to begin. The fragrance of the flowers and the warm, soft air from the summer breezes relaxed him. He was, at last, at peace with himself. Inwardly he prayed,

"Father in Heaven, thank you for preserving me through the fire of battle and giving me the peace and tranquility of this moment. Take care of me and my fellow officers and see us safely home."

The music started and was quite lovely. The dancers appeared and began to demonstrate their skills with numbers which included steps from Spain, Indian, Aztec, Mayan and current Mexican. They were colorfully dressed in quaint costumes of elaborate brocaded and beaded material. They whirled and stomped to the Latin music. The officers and their guests shouted greetings to them and some even ventured out to join the dancers on the floor. Jackson was enjoying the scene immensely and began to actually enter into the festivities. He had been drinking some exotic fruit punch. When one of his colleagues handed him a refill, he barely took notice of the exchange and proceeded to drink the second one. He began to feel a warm mesmerizing sensation as it spread throughout his body as he drained the glass and asked for another.

Without realizing it, Jackson was becoming tipsy from the punch. He began to watch the beautiful senoritas as they swayed to the music. He clapped his hands as they finished a number and stopped to rest. He had decided to go over and introduce himself to one particularly beautiful lady but as he bent over, he felt dizzy and his vision was blurred. Then he realized that he must have been drinking something with alcohol in it. He had violated his own rule, so he rose from his table, excused himself and retired to the hacienda feeling much guilt and remorse. Very few men would have felt like he did about drinking. They would have laughed it off and considered it a funny experience, but not Jackson. To him, it was a lapse in self control. He went to bed that night with a prayer on his lips, begging his Heavenly Father to forgive him for his transgression.

It was easy for Jackson to slip into a relaxed pattern of living. He liked a lot of the Mexican customs. Although it was hard to change his eating habits, he did...and for the better. He liked having his morning coffee and cakes in bed. He was unfamiliar with the late dinner they served but found that the afternoon tea would keep him from becoming hungry before dinner time. He would often take long walks just after tea time, visiting new friends and dignitaries. He liked to ride or walk down The Pasco, which was a wide road on the southwest edge of the city. He would meet and visit with his friends there as they sat beside the beautiful fountain.

Jackson often wrote Laura, describing to her the beautiful scenery and customs. He told her of his quest for religion and of his talks with the Catholic Priest. His determination to learn Spanish had led him to a serious study of the language. He spent most of his mornings deep in thought and when he was not on duty he would read or write in Spanish until he could master the vernacular. In due time, he was able to grasp the basics of the language and by ardent dedication, coupled with his ability to retain many

"Stonewall" Jackson during the Mexican War (1847)

J.B. Leib Photo, York, PA

69

of the Spanish drills, he began to practice his new tongue on the natives and the translators at Army Headquarters. He soon learned to read "Lord Chesterfield's Letters to his Son" and "Humboldt's History of Mexico" in Spanish.

In pursuing his search for a personal Church of his choice, Jackson felt that his religious beliefs should be coordinated with his own philosophy of God, The Father, Jesus Christ as man's link with Heaven and the mystical knot of Preordination. He studied the Old and New Testaments. Impressed with the prophets of old, he took note of the weakness and ills of mankind. He was troubled with the Judeo-Christian acceptance of Heaven and Hell and sought a church that fostered more of his philosophy in its mode of worship.

He discussed his search with some of his fellow officers, realizing that they belonged to the various church denominations. None were able to sway him to any particular form of Christianity. A thought occurred to him that perhaps he should investigate the Roman Catholic faith since he was in Mexico City where the Cardinal for the Church resided. He made an appointment with the Cardinal and spent several hours discussing, in Spanish, his problem. His Eminence advised Jackson to contact a certain Priest of the Church, Father Luis Hoya Alejandro, who would go into details of the religion and its worship.

Father Alejandro answered all of Jackson's questions and explained the religion. They met for several days with Jackson finally telling him that he wanted time to think over everything he had learned and he would then come to a decision. His decision, made about one week later, was that he would not join the Catholic Church as its philosphy was not as consistent as his and he felt he would not be comfortable in such a religious doctrine. He sent messages of thanks to the Cardinal and Father Alejandro for their time and effort. With that done, he temporarily suspended his search for a church.

Love came into Jackson's life when he met a beautiful senorita from one of the best known families in the city. He attended the officer's ball in the Hotel Nacional and here Don Miguel De La Casa, a relative of the Santiago family introduced him to Frederica De La-Costa Santiago.

"Senor Jackson, I am pleased to introduce my favorite cousin, Senorita Frederica De LaCosta," said Don Miguel.

Frederica extended her delicate, lace-gloved hand to Jackson who took it gently, saying, "I am honored to meet you, Senorita."

Lowering her eyes demurely she returned the greeting; her melodic voice intriguing Jackson.

She was a magnificent beauty with the blood of Spanish Castile and the aristocracy of Mexico in her veins. Jackson looked at the slender young beauty who had alabaster skin, dark sparkling eyes and black curly hair. Lieutenant Jackson was smitten with her fantastic beauty and her absolute charm!

The dashing Jackson, handsome in his American uniform, danced and conversed with Frederica all evening. When the ball was over, he asked her parents' permission to escort her home in the family carriage. Her Duenna stayed in the background, close by but out of sight, as was the custom.

The enclosed carriage moved sedately; the springs absorbing the rough road and cushioning the passengers' ride.

Hesitantly, Jackson initiated their conversation. "I am extremely flattered your parents allowed me to escort you home. I am privileged indeed."

"My parents hold you in high esteem. It is I who am flattered by your company," responded Frederica seriously. "Have you enjoyed your visit to our country?" she asked.

"Yes," answered Jackson. "I have found the countryside lovely, the people courteous and charming, and the customs appealing. I have grown to love the afternoon siestas and the languid pace," he continued.

Frederica smiled, a smile as soft and fleeting as a summer breeze. Jackson reveled in the warmth of her smile.

The ride home in the carriage was the most romantic thing Jackson had ever experienced! Pale moonlight and soft shadows filtered through the trees, casting its light on Frederica. She was so beautiful! He could see her graceful hands as she held her black lace shawl with one and brushed back a wispy curl with the other. He could feel her warmth as her soft body eased closer to him. He was intoxicated by the odor of her perfume. It was hard to talk about mundane things when all he wanted to do was gather her close and kiss those red lips.

The ride home was all too short. He would have lingered or perhaps walked in with her to talk more but the hour was late, and according to custom, the escort never ventured past the door. He would have to wait and follow their custom. He walked with her to the door, and with her Duenna trailing behind, stopped and kissed Frederica's soft hand.

"Senorita, I have had a wonderful evening with you. May I ask your parents' permission to see you again?"

"Ah, yes, Lieutenant, I, too, have had a wonderful evening. Do speak to my parents. You must come for a visit soon."

Jackson left the senorita with misgivings that he could not linger but with hope that he would see her again soon. When he went back to his quarters he was practically floating on air. It was hard to sleep for his thoughts were churning with excitement. He lay there and thought, "How beautiful my Frederica is! How sweet and wonderful was the time I spent with her." Never in his wildest imagination did he dream someone like her existed. He closed his eyes and saw her twinkling eyes and lips made for kisses. He knew he must wait for that until he knew her better. Sleep began to overtake him, but before it did, he offered a silent prayer to his Heavenly Father, thanking him for causing the meeting with Frederica!

The next day, Jackson sent a message to Frederica's parents asking permission to call on her. An answer came back through her Duenna that the Santiago family was leaving the following morning to visit family and friends in Tampico. They regretted he could not be received. Perhaps he could call on them in Tampico or in Mexico City when they returned in about two months. Jackson was heartsick that he would not be able to see her.

I could see that the love-smitten Lieutenant had nothing much on his mind but Frederica. He tried to get leave so he could travel to Tampico, but he had used up his leave for other furlough occasions and Headquarters would not grant any more. He did write Frederica a number of letters and she answered him promptly. He was full of hope, that when she returned, they could resume their friendship. But he was to be disappointed soon.

Frederica's letters dwindled down and finally stopped. He sat down at his desk and wrote a letter in which he poured his heart out to her. He told her how much he loved her and just what she meant to him. He wanted to be sure she knew he was serious about a romance and those first few hours together were meant to be more than just a casual meeting. He concluded his letter by requesting that she let him know whether or not their love was mutual or was it over. He'd never been one to pussyfoot around. He wanted to know where he stood.

Her answer finally arrived. She wrote him in Spanish and recalled their one and only meeting, pointing out that it was an evening she would long remember, but she was not sure she loved him as he loved her. Although she was very impressed with him, neither of them could be sure they were right for each other after just one meeting. Then she wrote him of meeting a man in Tampico who was the son of a Grandee from Barcelona, Spain. She had seen and been with him at numerous dinners, plays and social affairs in Tampico. Her parents approved of him and gave him permission to call on her. Their romance had been a short one when he asked for her hand. Her parents gave their consent and she felt certain their lives together would be blessed with happiness. She would be able to live in the manner to which she was accustomed and would be able to make visits to Mexico.

They would be married within the month. She ended her letter by telling Tom how much she admired him, his decency and honesty and was sure he was sincere. She said she hoped she had not misled him in any way and regretted any disappointment he might suffer as a result of the events. She knew she would, some day, hear great things about his accomplishments.

Jackson was crushed! He read the letter over and over as if he could not believe its contents. His one and only love affair had turned out to be disappointing and humiliating. He wondered if God had meant for this to happen. Was it one of those preordained events that somehow shadowed his life? Was he deserving of this? He walked around in a stupor for days. It was obvious to me that something had happened to him. I waited for him to tell me about it and one day, he did. After that, he seemed to straighten up and regain his senses. He reasoned that it would take some time to get over the love affair but he would, in the meantime, deal with things he knew about. Love was not one of them right now. I told him he had a whole life ahead of him and he would find someone else some day. Until then, he should get on with the business of soldiering!

Jackson tried to go on some mountain climbing trips with his friends, but he couldn't stand the rarefied atmosphere so he turned to long, overland hikes, often times camping out in the open and enjoying the clean air around the capitol of Mexico. This was excellent therapy for him.

We were waiting out the final terms of the Armistice. Everyone heard rumors that it would be soon. In the meantime, Jackson and I were in Captain Taylor's Battery which was a part of the Brigade of General Smith, Governor of the City. Jackson was drawing about ninety dollars per month and managed to save the greatest part of it. This would be a nice nest egg and would come in handy when he returned home.

On March 5, 1848, an Armistice was signed and a Treaty of Peace was ratified May 26, 1848. Troops began to evacuate the capitol. This was the end of an era for Jackson. One in which he had fought gallantly and heroically. He had attained the rank of Brevet Major, an accomplishment which filled him with pride. He had, indeed, built a future for himself in the Army.

General Taylor and his troops left Mexico and made their way home to Fort Hamilton, New York via New Orleans. Jackson and I were among the many happy men who made that last voyage over the Gulf of Mexico and then back up the Mississippi and Ohio Rivers toward the East Coast. There was a sadness hovering over the men as we made the journey, for so many of our comrades did not return with us. They had been killed in battle.

We often disccussed this fact, that it was a miracle we had made it through so many fierce battles without a wound.

"Surely, God had something to do with our good fortune. He must have a plan for us," Jackson said.

Fort Hamilton was a post that relaxed Major Jackson and his group. The first several months were spent sorting out the matters that had been deferred due to the Mexican War. During this time, he served on Court Martial duty at Carlisle Barracks, Pennsylvania and as Officer of the Day at the Fort Hamilton installation.

In early December of 1848, he was granted a furlough and visited his Uncle Cummins in Weston Mills. Although his uncle had kept up with his activities during the war, he was pleased to have Tom home again where he could hear about things first hand. He was anxious to know what Tom planned to do to further his career. They spent long hours talking about the battles. Tom told him about the strange country of Mexico, the beautiful flowers and exotic fruits and his uncle sat there listening to every word.

"Nephew, did you meet any of the beautiful senoritas?"

"Yes, I did. I went to some of the Mexican balls and danced with some of the most beautiful girls in the world. The homes were so magnificent." Then a frown crossed his face as he added,

"I fell in love with one of them....wanted to marry her but she left for a two month visit and met someone else while she was there."

Cummins could see that he was upset over the love affair. He tried to console him as best he could.

"You have plenty of years to find a wife. All of us have disappointments like yours at some time in life. Yours just came early. Don't you worry, some fine lady will come along in due time."

The discussion was dropped and never mentioned again. Cummins decided it would be best to let Tom get over it in his own way.

Tom stayed with his uncle for one half of his furlough and then went to Beverly to be with Laura and her family. By the time he reached the little town, the first snowfall of the season had come. As he stepped off the stage, he could see that Beverly had been turned into a winter wonderland. This was a far cry from the heat of Mexico. He was glad to be back where he could experience Christmas with snow.

Laura and Will met him and took him home in the carriage. The warm lap robes covered their legs as they made their way over the frozen, snow covered road to their home. The familiar clop, clop of the horses' feet, as they sped along, was music to Tom's ears. He had been away so long, he'd almost forgotten what it sounded like to ride through snow.

"Tom, we want to hear all about the war. I have waited so long to hear the details from your lips. You promised you would tell us about it and we're holding you to your word."

"I'll tell you all about it, Laura. You would like Mexico and all of its beauty."

They rode down the long lane toward the house. Tom could see the children standing at the window, just watching for them. They bounded out of the house and into his arms when they pulled up.

"My Nancy, how you have grown!"

"And, Will, you are almost a young man, so tall and handsome!" He kissed Nancy and extended his hand to Will who was so pleased to be considered a man instead of a child.

The deepening shadows of an early winter afternoon had begun to cast a haze over the snow covered countryside. When they opened the front door, Tom could see that the home had already been decorated for Christmas. Inside, a roaring fire gave a warm glow to the beautiful parlor. He could hardly believe it was nearly Christmas and he had made it to his loved ones in time. It had been many years since he had celebrated the joyous holiday of Christmas with his sister and members of the family.

"Tom, you know where your room is. Go up and unpack, then come down here where we can sit around the fire and talk!"

Tom went upstairs where the house boy had taken his bags. He entered the room and saw that everything was ready for him. A fire blazed in the stone fireplace, the oil lamps were burning and there was hot water in the pitcher on the wash stand. He quickly unpacked, washed up and changed clothes. Although he had become accustomed to wearing a uniform, it was good to be able to change to civilian clothes and become a member of the family again. He began to relax.

The family was waiting for him when he walked into the room. Nancy and Will listened as he talked about his war experiences. Every few minutes, Laura would ask another question. She had kept all of his letters and had made mental notes about certain instances.

A gong sounded heralding the supper hours. They went into the dining room to enjoy a welcome home feast. Laura had ordered Tom's favorite dishes to be prepared.

"This is wonderful food. I haven't had home cooking like this since I left the farm. Mexico's dishes were good, but very spicy and hot. Actually, my main diet consisted of their bread and many kinds of fruit."

"Well, we need to get you on a better diet, Tom."

"I did gain weight after the war ended as I lived in luxury! The owner of the hacienda, where we were quartered, fed us well. Also, we went to so many banquets and balls where we had to eat or hurt the feelings of our hosts. We could not offend those we had conquered. They are a proud nation and it was hard for them to accept defeat!"

With supper over, the family went back to the parlor to resume their very spirited conversation. Everyone was so engrossed in Tom's tales of the war, they didn't realize how late it was. So he called a halt to the questions to enable the family to get some rest!

The remaining days before Christmas were spent getting ready for the event. The children were busy stringing popcorn to be used as garland on the tree. Bright red cranberries were also strung while Laura fashioned ornaments out of bits of colorful cloth and beads. Will brought home the multi colored tin candle holders and matching small candles which would be clipped on the Christmas tree as the final touch. They would be lighted on Christmas eve and again on Christmas morning. The beautiful angel with her feathery wings was put on the top of the tree just below the glittering star which was on the topmost branch.

The long sideboard in the dining room was heavy with fruitcake, pies and candy. The cut glass punch bowl with its matching ladle was placed in the center just ready to be filled with Will's finest eggnog on Christmas afternoon when they would have their annual open house for friends and neighbors.

Tom was pleased that Laura had carried the tradition of open house on Christmas Day. This was something she learned from Uncle Cummins who always had open house in Weston Mills.

"What can I do to help, Laura?"

"You and Will can decorate the stair-rail and mantle with the garlands of holly. Be sure to put the mistletoe over the door. That is for good luck and who knows, you might meet some nice young lady by New Year's Eve who will walk under that mistletoe!"

Tom had not told Laura about his sad love affair. At this point, he doubted if he would ever want to kiss a woman again.

Tom had brought each of the family special presents from Mexico. They were carefully wrapped and placed under the tree to be opened on Christmas morning. Nancy and Will were so excited as Christmas eve came. They had supper and dressed in their great coats in preparation for their ride to the church for Christmas Eve services. Tom looked forward to this. It had been a long time since he had attended a Protestant service.

Jackson later told me that what he treasured most was the Holy Bible Laura gave him that Christmas. He carried it with him for the rest of his life and he became so thoroughly knowledgeable with its contents that it helped him decide on a religious faith. He carried it throughout his many battles and every place he went.

Following Christmas and his pleasant reunion with Laura and her family, Tom left to visit a friend, Peter Conrad, who resided some twenty miles south of Beverly. He enjoyed his visit with his friend but the weather was cold and rainy. He caught a severe cold and decided to double back to Weston Mills for one of his uncle's "old cold treatments." He used the remedy and let Aunt Mary wait on him for a few days. She urged him to stay in bed and let her fix him some of her chicken soup.

"Don' nobody wait on dat chile' but me while he's sick. I done nursed him through many a sick spell and ah'll git him well dis' time." She delighted in the opportunity to fuss over him.

Tom felt better by the end of the week and despite Aunt Mary's warnings, he traveled by horseback to Hot Springs, Virginia on his way to Richmond. He called on John S. Carlile, the State Senator from his district and discussed the Mexican War with him. He also talked about the economic situation in Virginia and his prospects for becoming a career army officer. The Senator listened attentively to what Jackson had to say for several reasons. The Jackson family, headed by Cummins represented substantial power. He could be counted on, in much of Carlile's district, for a good part of the district votes. Major Jackson was a genuine war hero having been promoted rapidly and decorated for bravery and cited in public for his achievements by Commanding General, Winfield Scott. The Senator made notes for his files, keeping in mind that this young Major might someday, be someone of importance. He promised Tom he would keep him informed should he hear or learn of any news that may have a bearing on his situation. Tom left the Senator's office with a good feeling...one that he had enlisted his friendship and might one day, reap some benefit as a result of the meeting. Jackson left the very next day for Fort Hamilton, New York.

New Year's Day, 1849, was spent back in his quarters. He entered in his personal log, a detailed account of where and how he spent his furlough. Then he wrote letters to Laura, Peter Conrad, Uncle Cummins and the Senator. He resolved that for 1849, his first objective was to finalize his intention of finding and joining a church. That would satisfy his thirst for his own personal beliefs and convictions. His will to find what he wanted in a church was stronger than ever!

Chapter 6

Brevet Major Thomas Jackson continued his search for a religion he could follow. He had examined many faiths so far and had yet to feel comfortable with any of them. He realized that he had become confused over their differences but it did not alter his intense desire to search until he found the right one. He was very impressed with his Commanding Officer's religious beliefs. He and the Commandant had often talked about the Bible, God, and Colonel Taylor's interpretation of his belief. Jackson was impressed with Taylor's knowledge of the Bible.

The Chaplain of the post, Reverend Parks was an alumnus of West Point and was well known as a Christian scholar. Parks had given up his life as an officer and became a Minister in the Episcopal Church. Jackson felt he might attain his personal salvation through baptism in the Episcopal Church. Colonel Taylor had talked with him at length, pointing out that Episcopal communion might be the answer to Jackson's dilemma.

The Episcopal faith appeared to Jackson as an Evangelical system and he refused to accept some of its dogmatic features as founded in Scriptural law. He made it plain that if he obtained baptism in the Episcopal Church, it would be on the basis of the Catholic Body of Christ and not as a member of the Episcopal denomination. He did, however, agree to accept in the dogma of the Episcopal church, the name and belief of the Redeemer, who, he hoped, had saved him. With this understanding, Rev. Parks baptized him into communion at St. Johns Episcopal Chapel, Fort Hamilton, New York, on April 29, 1849. Sponsors for Jackson's baptism were Colonels Dimick and Taylor. Major Jackson was pleased but still held the nagging question in the back of his mind,

"Will this be my personal salvation?"

With his Baptism out of the way, Jackson turned his mind back to military matters. Daily tasks at the post were routine drills and Artillery practice. They were regularly scheduled tasks that were closely supervised with rigor and stern vigilance. Every gun, caisson, support wagon, horse and rider were inspected closely for any infraction of regulations. Jackson contended that even on a peace footing, all branches of the military should be adequately prepared so that men, horses and equipment would be able to move on a moment's notice. He was building an excellent record for himself. Colonel Taylor took note of the thoroughness with which Jackson handled his troops and drills.

At the end of November, 1849, Jackson spent a week at Carlisle, Pennsylvania on Court Martial duty. This was the third such trip he had made in connection with courts martials. He also decided that a trip back to Richmond following his duty in Carlisle, would be an excellent opportunity to keep his name current in certain political circles. Everything that he did in this respect was in keeping with his status as a United States Army officer. At no time did he ever violate Army regulations concerning relations with civilians in political office. His purpose in going to Richmond was to learn from John S. Carlile whether the senator had heard of any new opportunities which might concern Jackson. While in Richmond, he met a future Governor of Virginia, Mr. Letcher, who asked him if he intended to make the military his career. Jackson replied,

"I shall remain in the army and at present have no plans to do anything else. Naturally, Sir, if some opportunity should develop, outside of army service, I would be most interested in listening to whatever you or your associates have to offer and I would give you a prompt reply."

He returned to Fort Hamilton around the first part of 1850. The Army doctors made their annual physical examinations and found that he had gained some 33 pounds over the past year. They suggested he eat less and exercise more. They were aware of his dyspepsia since he had suffered flare ups from his first day at West Point. They also knew he was a hypochrondriac and had many imaginary ailments. His eccentric ideas concerning health were well known; such as his belief that holding his left arm above his head, several times a day, would improve circulation, and washing with cold water, the first thing in the morning would improve his stimulation of the brain. They took note of these facts and said nothing regarding them. Instead, they put him on a diet and exercise routine which he followed as if it was a manual of regulations.

The Major was assigned again to a trial court at Plattsburg Barracks, New York in May of 1850. Each time he served as a member of a Court Martial, he gained invaluable information as to what violations soldiers normally were charged with. No two cases were alike and Jackson took to heart each soldier's case. He followed Army regulations and tried to be fair in each verdict. Some cases were terribly difficult to decide and before he gave out his vote, he would wrestle with his conscience to satisfy himself that his decision was correct and just.

He was soon recognized as an experienced and well respected Court Martial officer for later on in August of 1850, he was called to serve in a trial to be held at Fort Niagara, in Oswego, New York. Some time after this, Jackson returned to stay at a water cure establishment in Oswego where they used the "wet sheet" treatment to cure dyspepsia.

On September 3, 1850, he returned to West Point, where he was assigned for Court Martial duty. He found many changes in the place. Few of his former comrades were there and despite the nostalgia he felt, he realized that things are never quite the same after one has left. He was there to do a job. The army expected a fair and speedy Court Martial trial and he would see to it that things moved rapidly and justly to whatever decision was made. Once again, his prestige was enhanced by the rapidity of the trial and the verdict was accepted by all parties as fair.

News came in early October that the company would be moving from Fort Hamilton. It was rumored that Florida would be their destination. Jackson quickly asked for and was given a furlough so he could spend a week with his family in Beverly and Weston Mills. It was a peaceful and relaxing time spent in Virginia where the trees had turned to colors of red and yellow. He spent long hours talking with Laura and Will, then on to Weston Mills where he visited his uncle. None of them realized that this farewell would be his last. He would not be in a position to return.

Jackson had just returned from his leave when orders came through to proceed to Fort Meade, Florida, about fifty miles inland from Tampa. He knew this country was considered a frontier and they were being sent to preserve the peace. Many of the Seminole Indians had been moved out of the area but some remained and were considered a threat against the white settlers.

Fort Meade was a desolate post in a land replete with lakes, rivers, and meandering streams. Wild animals roamed and snakes slithered through the camp underbrush. It was a Godforsaken area and the men didn't like duty there. There was constant bickering and dissatisfaction in the ranks. The officers were forced to bear down on the men because they had to be in a constant state of alertness. It was dangerous country where anything might happen. Jackson had been forewarned to be on guard against everything!

Because of army regulations in peace time, Jackson's rank was Lieutenant instead of Major. The officer commanding the post was Captain W. H. French who was also a former Brevet Major like Jackson. They had met before when they served in the Mexican war and renewed their friendship at Fort Meade.

French installed Lt. Jackson in charge of the commissary and appointed him Quartermaster for the post. These were new posts for Jackson but he eagerly filled both. Both French and Jackson were ambitious. French, in particular, wanted to impress the District's Commanding General with his administration of Fort Meade. He became rather "picky" with Jackson and the rest of the men, despite the fact that Jackson and the others were doing a good job. French wrote letters to the General in which he praised himself and pointed out how well he personally conducted scouting parties and maintained discipline and order. He took credit for eliminating drunkenness at Fort Meade and brought attention to the fact that he had built additional living quarters so the men could bring their families in and live on the post.

French's ambition never seemed to end. He went so far as to assume certain duties including some of Jackson's Commissary operations and Quartermaster tasks. Jackson felt that French had gone too far in assuming some of his duties since army regulations spelled out the rights, duties and privileges of a Quartermaster and Supply Officer in a garrison post. He let French know that he was interfering and demanded an independence which French resented. This type of interference set the stage for bickering and unresolved quarreling that lasted through Jackson's entire term of duty at Fort Meade. He always felt that he was equal to French in rank since they both left the Mexican War as Brevet Majors and he made it very clear to French that they were on an "equal rank" basis. This was a fact French couldn't deny.

French made it clear that he expected Lieutenant Jackson to show deference to him beacuse he was the Post Commander and could not tolerate a subordinate who refused to recognize his superior position. This incensed Jackson. Thus the two men found themselves in a situation where both ambitious officers developed an intense rivalry for their individual accomplishments, all because they wanted future recognition and promotion to a higher rank.

The Jackson-French quarrel did not soften or abate. On the contrary, they battled each other fiercely on the matter of public buildings to be erected on the post. Jackson complained to Department Headquarters in a letter, stating,

"Captain and Brevet Major, W.H. French, First Artillery has denied me; by informing me that I have no control whatsoever over the construction of the buildings."

I was still Jackson's assistant, working side by side with him and I could see that the situation between the two men was rapidly deteriorating. Jackson began to ignore his superior officer when he passed him. This angered French more and to the point of considering charging him with insubordination. The entire garrison felt the hostility between the two. Morale fell and discipline was at a low point. Realizing how badly the post was suffering because of their differences, Jackson stopped French one day and told him how hurt he was over the situation. He added that he could not understand why French acted the way he did unless it was because of his personal dislike for him. French denied the statement and tried to console Jackson by saying Jackson had misunderstood his actions and dislike had nothing to do with it. He told Jackson that if he felt like he was being mistreated, he should write a letter of complaint to a higher authority, and he, French, would willingly forward such a complaint to the District Commanding General.

Jackson decided to write the letter, setting forth the basis of his complaint and asked for a decision on whether or not his Commanding Officer had usurped authority. He made no mention of any personal differences between himself and French. French endorsed Jackson's letter and enclosed one of his own to Headquarters in which he told an entirely different story. He reported that Jackson was "trying to assume to himself, more importance than the Commandant of the Post." The more French wrote, the angrier he got. He made reference to the many things that occurred, Jackson's impertinence, insubordination and his relationship with the Junior Officers at the Post and last, his bad influence on the morale of the men in the ranks. Obviously, the Commanding General could not take a stand favoring Jackson's request since a general order existed covering the situation.

French's letter accomplished its purpose. Jackson drew a reprimand from the Commanding General. The General stated,

"The Quartermaster Post was under the orders of the Commandant and the Commandant was responsible for everything done at the post. He was the one who would get the blame for failure. The Staff Officer, as expressed in orders No. 13, is emphatically his Assistant." The Commanding General added,

"A difference of opinion amongst officers may honestly occur on points of duty. It ought never to degenerate into personalities or to be considered a just cause for withholding the common courtesies of life so essential in an officer and to the happiness and quiet of garrison life."

Jackson was obviously disappointed in the answer he received. He particularly noticed the remark about "personalities" and understood by that term, what French must have said to the Commanding General when he sent Jackson's letter to the Commander. French had taken advantage of his position as Commandant. This was not a surprise but certainly unfair.

Jackson's dyspepsia worsened as the unending feud continued. He felt he had been treated unfairly and such treatment was inconsistent with his beliefs on morality, fairness and principle. He began to crack under the strain. By early spring, his eyes became affected and weakened. He became ill with severe stomach pains and the doctors put him on sick call. Eventually they took him off the active list because of his debilitating condition. He called me into his tent,

"Sergeant Sparks, I am bored with this inactivity. I have nothing to do but sit and think about the situation. Tell me, how are things in the Quartermaster headquarters?"

"Well, Sir, they are doing fine. We are under the orders of Captain French. I'm sorry, sir, that you find yourself idle. Wish I could do something about it."

"Thank you, Sergeant, but there's nothing anyone can do."

I could see that he was sinking into a depression and this worried me for I had seen him get like this before. Hate was burning him up. All I could hope for was some miracle which would straighten him out.

Jackson spent his time praying for guidance, reading his Bible and writing to Laura. In one of his letters to her, he wrote:

"You say that I must live on the past fame for the present. I say not only for the present but during life. In regard to leaving the army, no, it's doubtful whether I shall relinquish the military profession as I am very partial to it."

When he wrote about French, he said,

"A hypocrite is, in my judgement, one of the most detestable of beings. My opinion is that everyone should honestly and carefully investigate the

Bible and then, if he can believe It, to be the Word of God, to follow His teachings.''

Jackson was an observant Christian, and a staunch believer in upholding religious morals. A situation that he noted at Fort Meade involving Captain French and a nurse named Julia who worked in his home, was becoming the subject of camp gossip. They were saying that ''Julia's boy-friends had best stay away from the Major's home as the Major had taken her for himself.'' French did not act discreet enough to stay out of the gossip situation. Fort Meade was a small installation and the news traveled fast!

French was seen walking with Julia and on one occasion, far from the post. Some of the soldiers saw the two heading toward a wooded area. Tongues wagged and the information reached Jackson soon. This was an embarrassing situation for French and Jackson saw it as a breach of Christian morals, a violation of army rules and regulations, and a violation of code of conduct regarding officers and their wives. He thought French's conduct should not be tolerated and here was an opportunity for him to get back at his adversary.

A number of soldiers paid a visit to Jackson to give their version of French's affair with the servant girl. If such stories were true then French was not conducting himself as an officer and a gentleman. There was, however, not enough evidence to warrant charges against French for no one had actually seen him do anything unbecoming to an officer's status. All of the rumors were speculation. Jackson thought about this situation for a while then he asked questions of the soldiers carefully planting the seeds of speculation and doubt in to their minds, to the point they went to their Sergeant and told him what had occurred. The Sergeant went to French and told him what was being said; in turn French became so angry at Jackson for stirring up trouble, he had Jackson arrested for ''conduct unbecoming an officer and a gentleman.'' With this twist of events, the post was brimming with rumors again. A nasty situation for all concerned which affected morale on the post.

Charges and counter charges ensued. Reams of paper were sent to headquarters with conflicting statements by French and Jackson.

Jackson's appraisal of French made it appear that ''French was a harsh, quick-spoken officer, with an overwhelming dedication to his own advancement to trivia and appearances. He was also at the same time, a man who is not to be believed as speaking the truth and therefore, in his opinion, requires him to speak falsely.''

Since he was confined to quarters, he had more time to prepare other charges, such as those where French had used his authority to restrict him, to show prejudice in ordering discipline on the post and unbecoming conduct.

All of these charges seemed trivial but they were indicative of Jackson's resentment.

I knew Jackson had carried his hate of French too far when French became concerned with Jackson's charges of moral degeneracy, attacks on his personal character and damaging his name in the army. French disclaimed Jackson's story and said ''that Jackson had no real evidence pointing to anything else but his vindictiveness and rash charges.''

Jackson retaliated with counter charges stating that he realized how weak his case looked and urged that a Court of Inquiry be called to investigate the Fort Meade situation. He said, ''much more could be charged against the Post Commander.'' This was a rather vague statement even though Jackson was sure the court would find that French was not above intimidating witnesses if he had the chance.

French favored a Court Martial of Jackson over a Court of Inquiry. He felt this would be a way of stopping as well as discrediting Jackson and his charges against him. He also felt that Jackson should be tried for actions unbecoming an officer and for incorrect conduct as well as slandering his superior officer by the method used in questioning the men on the post, thus causing a decline in morale and discipline at the Fort. He requested the court be held at Fort Meade because all of the evidence was there. Jackson disagreed with this request because ''he wanted to clear himself and did not think it could be done fairly at Fort Meade since French's influence there was so great it would have a strong tendency to defeat the ends of justice.''

David E. Twiggs, Major General, Commanding became very displeased with the charges and counter charges that were piled up at headquarters. He read through the documents and decided the matter was ridiculous. How two Brevet majors could act like this was beyond his comprehension so he ordered French to release Jackson; then he ordered the Court of Inquiry application be rejected.

French considered Twiggs' decision as a reprimand and appealed the case. Twiggs responded by writing to Washington recommending that French's appeal be denied. General Winfield Scott upheld Twiggs' decision. As a result, French became hysterical and continued making charges to such an extent that General Twiggs ordered French transferred to Fort Myers and placed under command of the officer of that Post.

Having lost his Fort Meade command, French appealed the case to the Secretary of War. This was an obvious mistake since his appeal had to go through General Twiggs' office. Twiggs was fed up with French's attitude and his inability to accept the original decision that had been handed down in the case. As a result, Twiggs submitted the following note attached to French's appeal.

"I deem it necessary only to say that I have found no reason to regret the transfer of Major French to Fort Myers. Such transfer had, in my judgement, been rendered necessary by the fact that Major French had preferred charges successively against all the officers serving under his orders, and had shown himself incapable of conducting the service harmoniously at a detached post." General in-Chief Scott, General Twiggs and their staffs had reviewed the papers and reached the same decision. The Secretary of War, C. M. Conrad, commented; "I perceive nothing in this case that calls for my interference."

French lost his independent command and henceforth was to be a subordinate in the other army posts at which he was stationed. It was a bitter lesson and loss to him, one from which he would never recover. His record was stained as a result of too much pride, obstinacy and a failure to exercise good judgment.

Jackson had applied for extended sick leave during his troubles with French but was unable to take any of it during the period because he was under house arrest. Finally, he left Fort Meade on May 21, 1851. He had suffered a blow to his pride and disappointment over his subordinate position. He had to face up to distorted questions of duty and morality and had met them head on. His honesty and perseverance again showed off his character. Decency and morality were so deeply ingrained in him that nothing, not even the possibility of jeopardizing his military career, stood in the way of his distinguishing right from wrong. He had met the challenges, unpleasant as they were, realizing they might cast a shadow over his army career, and had survived them. Now that he was leaving Florida, he was determined to concentrate on the future of his career. He had to decide whether he would continue to be in the army or move into civilian life.

During all of the stress and turmoil at Fort Meade, Jackson had received an inquiry from Colonel F. H. Smith, Superintendent of Virginia Military Institute at Lexington, Virginia, regarding his possible interest in a teaching position there as a Professor of Natural and Experimental Philosophy and Artillery Tactics. Colonel Smith wrote his letter on February 4, 1851 at the suggestion of Major Daniel H. Hill. The salary for the position would be $1200.00 a year.

Despite the difficulties facing Jackson at that time, he yearned for a change of scenery and particularly one that would take him out of the contentious atmosphere of the Florida situation. He thought the serene and peaceful setting in the Shenandoah Valley would be a most welcome exchange for the hot, damp and swampy country around Fort Meade. He gave the offer serious thought before answering.

Jackson wrote Colonel Smith on February 25, 1851 expressing his interest in the position. He requested his name be presented to the Board of Visitors for consideration. Perhaps it was an act of fate but on March 17, 1851, John S. Carlile, a lawyer from Beverly, the home of Jackson's sister, Laura, and a good friend of Jackson, was appointed a member of the V.M.I. Board of Visitors.

In a letter written to Laura about the offer, Jackson said, "I consider the position both conspicuous and desirable. I will be within 150-160 miles of you!"

Meanwhile Jackson waited for Colonel Smith's answer, realizing full well that a great many things could go wrong and there was no reason to become overly anxious about the board's final decision. He knew there would be other candidates applying for the post and a certain amount of politics would be involved. He took his fatalistic attitude that what would be, would come to pass if it was God's will.

A lot of powerful forces were at work on the V.M.I. appointment. A group headed by John S. Carlile and Major D. H. Hill spoke very highly of Jackson and presented recommendation of leading citizens of the State as well as making reference to his brilliant Mexican War record attesting to the desirability of appointing him to the position. After due deliberation, discussion and examination of all candidates and their records, the Board of Visitors unanimously chose Major Jackson on March 27, 1851, for the post. The forces of Carlile and Hill were highly gratified that their recommended candidate won out over all the others. The Board of Visitors were pleased to obtain a man of such sterling character who was imbued with the highest of Christian ethics, tempered in the fire of war and rounded with military skills and leadership. He was a true war hero as was evidenced by his record.

Colonel Smith wrote Jackson the next day, March 28, 1851 as follows;

"Sir, it gives me pleasure to inform you that you were, yesterday, unanimously elected Professor of Natural Experimental Philosophy and Artillery Tactics in the Virginia Military Institute, with a salary of $1,200, and an allowance of $120, per annum for quarters until a suitable house can be erected for you.

"It is the wish of the Board that you report for duty by the 1st day of July. Your pay and prerequisites to commence from the date of your reporting for duty. It will be well for you to come on as soon as possible, that you may make use of the opportunity afforded in the revision of the course of Nat. Phil. by Major Gilham, who now fills the chair and will be transferred to the Chemical Dept. by your appointment, to prepare yourself for the duties of the next session.

Our Board meets at Lexington on the 25th of June and I deem it of great importance that you meet them at that time. With this view, I shall forward immediately to Washington and make application in your behalf, for a furlough of 6 months. I think I may be able to obtain this favor to the Institute from the War Department and should it be granted, you can use it or not as you see proper.

I am, very respectfully,

Francis H. Smith, Supt. V.M.I.

Be pleased to let me hear from you immediately directed to Lexington, Va.''

Sufficient to say, Jackson was jubilant on receiving news of his appointment. At last, a concern which occupied his mind for so long, was now resolved. He could make plans as to how his leave would be spent. He sat down to answer Colonel Smith.

"Fort Meade, Florida
April 22, 1851

Colonel,

Your letter of the 28th inst, informing me that I have been elected Professor of Natural and Experimental Philosophy and Artillery Tactics in the Virginia Military Institute, has been received.

The high honor conferred by the Board of Visitors, in selecting me unanimously, to fill such a professorship, gratified me exceedingly. I hope to be able to meet the Board on the 25th of June next but fear that circumstances over which I have no control, will prevent my doing so before that time.

For your kindness in endeavoring to procure me a leave of absence for six months, as well as for the interest you have otherwise manifested in my behalf, I feel under strong and lasting obligations. Should I desire a furlough of more than one month commencing on the 1st of July next, it would be for the purpose of visiting Europe.

I regret that recent illness has prevented my giving you an earlier answer. Any communication you may have to make, previous to the 1st of June, please direct to this place.

I am, very respectfully, your obedient servant.

T. J. Jackson"

To Jackson, it was apparent that his appointment, like so many other events in his life, seemed to have been tinged with Predestination, in which he had so much faith. The God in whom he had placed his trust, had not let him down. Was this an omen of things to come?

Filled with enthusiasm, he wrote Laura on April 22, 1851.

"Good news. I have been elected to the Professorship at The Virginia Military Institute and you may expect me home in the latter part of June."

The news of Tom's appointment had reached Laura earlier by a message received from John S. Carlile, who as a friend of the family, had worked so diligently for Jackson's appointment.

Laura and the family were elated with the welcome news. Tom would be back from Florida and everyone would have an opportunity to visit with him. Furthermore, he would not be too far from her when he taught at V.M.I. The world had, indeed, taken on a brighter hue for Laura.

Jackson made preparations in May of 1851 to leave Florida. His nine month requested furlough had been granted and after cleaning up his affairs at Fort Meade, he departed for home and his new career.

After a visit with Laura and her family, Uncle Cummins in Weston Mills and some of his friends, he went back to New York to make contact with Dr. Lowry Barney of Henderson, New York.

Dr. Barney was noted for his treatment of dyspepsia and since Jackson had long been troubled with the complaint, he decided to seek Dr. Barney's help. He went to see him and the good Doctor suggested he stay at his home for six weeks and take the treatment.

The diet for dyspepsia consisted of cornbread and buttermilk, supplemented with fresh fruit. Mrs. Barney prepared the meals which Jackson enjoyed. His daily regimen consisted of long walks in the beautiful countryside. He drank water from Lake Ontario and did it often enough to warrant keeping his cup at hand near the Lake. He felt himself rejuvenated by the good food, peace and quiet of the cool woods and the sparkling lake, and the opportunity to visit points of interest around Henderson Harbor. His health improved considerably as a result of the treatment.

Some of Jackson's new found friends described him as a tall, slender and very courtly man who often talked of his Mexican War Campaigns and asked many questions about Henderson and the territory. They said the Major was very polite, God fearing and had a mystique about him that left a first time visitor impressed with the absolute determination of the man, to succeed at whatever he attempted. They thought he was a man to be reckoned with when events ever reached a point of decision.

Chapter 7

Jackson's health was much improved after his six weeks in the home of Dr. Barney. He was fit again, weighing much less than he had, yet feeling better than he had in years. His dyspepsia had disappeared, at least for the time being, and he was careful to follow the diet for fear his malady would return. His composure had returned and for this he was thankful. Now he felt he could face V.M.I. and his new career with confidence.

On August 13, 1851, Major Thomas Jackson reported to the Virginia Military Institute and was assigned to duty at once. He found the Cadet Corps preparing for summer drill and encampment. Since Major William Gilham, the regular Commandant of Cadets was absent, Jackson was temporarily assigned as Commandant.

There was a great contrast in personalities of the two men. Gilham, Old Gil, as he was known to the Cadets, had a high shrill voice and his actions were quick and restless. Discipline under Gilham was a must. No one knew Jackson yet so he was the subject of much curiosity to the Corps. When they marched past Jackson, for the first time, they looked at the Major in wonder. He was dressed in a Virginia Militia uniform of a double breasted, blue coat, white pants, white gloves, and his enormous feet were encased in worn but well blacked artillery boots. His head was topped with a new cap. Needless to say, his appearance was rather incongruous and quite uncommon for a V.M.I. professor. One could hear much suppressed and muffled laughter among the Cadets as they marched by.

Tom Mumford, the Cadet Adjutant, had been appointed as Jackson's aide. He advised Jackson of the usual daily routine which was to give daily orders to the Corps, plan its events and establish the drill and instruction routine. He listened to Mumford and quickly asked for a copy of the Cadet Regulations.

Jackson read the regulations and commented to Mumford that many of the routines had similarities to those used at West Point. It was very clear to the Corps that Jackson's methods and ideas were to be followed. They found they couldn't put anything over on him for he accepted no excuses for failure to carry out orders. Punishment for regulations infractions was carried out speedily. He would brook no insubordination or disrespect and even resorted to Courts Martials as a means of enforcing order and discipline. He was not like Gilham for he was painfully exacting in details and precision in his commands. The Corps knew, unmistakably, what was meant.

Mumford perceived Jackson to be a man full of contradictions. "No two men could be more unlike than Major Jackson in repose and Major Jackson in action. When he would give the command to the cannoneers to fire, the ring of that voice was clear enough to be heard and to burn amid the rumbling of the wheels, giving life and nerve to the holder of the lanyard. Yet, Jackson in repose was a man whose brow appeared inanimate and almost drooping. Then to spring into action on a moment's notice and his whole countenance would change before your eyes to the figure of a soldier who was conscious of power and had been inspired."

In September 1851, Major Jackson led the Corps of cadets on a march to Rock Bridge Alum Springs, Bath Alum Springs and Warm Springs. It was on this trip that the cadets became considerably aware of the Major's insistence on attention to small details. No matter how small the problem, they learned that once an objective was set, he expected a follow through to a solution within the time structure set by him. No deviations or departures from the original project would be brooked. The cadets were often upset by his methods of teaching but they did learn the lesson and stored their knowledge for future use.

The cadets returned to the school in late September, in time for the opening of the academic semester. Jackson moved into the new barracks on the 24th, rooming on the third stoop with Major Gilham as his roommate.

Jackson was assigned to teach the second class Optics and Analytical Mechanics, first class Optics, Acoustics and Astronomy. These courses presented a real problem for him because he was unfamiliar with each subject. He spent long hours studying the material in preparation for classes. His bad eyesight caused him much trouble, thus he had to commit each day's lesson to memory. He established a routine of making use of the limited daylight left after the last class in the afternoon. He took this time to hastily read the next day's material and committing it to memory. The evenings were spent in going over, in his mind, the lesson for the next day. His practice was to stand bolt upright or sit rigidly erect, facing the wall and rehash or commit to memory, everything he could about the lesson. He had used this procedure during his days at West Point. His powers of concentration and his photographic memory were now being put to good use.

Jackson was not a good classroom teacher. He found it hard to explain the subjects such as Optics and Analytical Mechanics. The cadets sensed that their professor was not personally exuberant about each course and as a result they mocked him, made jeering remarks and called him names. "Old Tom Fool is stuck again!" was whispered behind his back as they jeered at him.

Despite the Professor's discipline, the cadets created episodes which bordered on violation of cadet regulations pertaining to respect and obedience toward any superior officer. One, Major W. N. Marcer and one of the cadets who studied under Jackson, later wrote,

"I often look backward and wonder at the great patience of Major Jackson under the fire of some mischievous cadet, seeking to irritate or annoy him during lecture hours!"

"The lecture room was surrounded by the sleeping quarters of the cadets. This made it convenient for them to indulge in pranks then scurry to their holes with little or no chance of detection. I frequently saw the Major lecturing his class on some subject and some mischievous cadet would be shooting water at the professor by means of a syringe through a knot hole in the door. Frequently in the Artillery class, I saw the cadets acting as horses to limber chest and caisson, run away in mimic fright and often scatter the watching crowds of ladies and gentlemen, while the Major was yelling himself hoarse in vain, endeavoring to check them."

It was about this time that I came back into Major Jackson's life again. I had not seen him since we left Florida. I applied for and was accepted as an instructor in Artillery Gunnery at V.M.I. and was happy to find that I was to be Jackson's aide. Both of us were pleased over the arrangement.

It did not take long for me to size up the situation and know that Jackson was working under a strain. I realized he didn't know the subject matter of his courses and I could see that he was using his West Point methods to get his lessons prepared. What I didn't foresee was the trouble he was having with discipline of the cadets. After working with him a few weeks and watching him teach, I realized that he was dealing with a totally different caliber of men and this is where the trouble began.

The V.M.I. cadets came from some of the finest families in Virginia, representing wealth, culture, and ancestry dating back to pre-Revolutionary days. The world looked bright and promising to the proud group of happy-go-

"Stonewall" Jackson as an instructor at VMI (c. 1851)

J.B. Leib Photo, York, PA

lucky Virginians. Their joie de vivre knew no bounds. On the other hand, they were attending classes taught by a war seasoned military officer who had worked and fought under the strictest military conditions, where discipline was of the utmost importance. Also, the soldiers in Jackson's troops, were not from the elite but reprsented a cross section of the country from the very poor to the rich. Jackson had not been faced with such insubordination or lack of discipline. He did expect everyone to act as they did in the army.

I decided to use the bounds of our old friendship and talk with the Major. I advised him of what, I had concluded, was the problem.

"Major, you must consider that these young men are not professional soldiers such as you commanded in the army or on the battlefields of Mexico. They come from distinguished Virginia families and are the flower of some of our native aristocracy. You will undoubtedly succeed with them if you exercise some restraint in your discipline and enforcement of regulations until you have become accustomed to them and they to you."

I could see that while I talked, the Major cooly and calmly listened to every word I said without interruption, evaluating his answer before replying,

"Caleb, it is our duty and responsibility to train these men so that they will ultimately leave here with the finest military education we can give them. They must be prepared so that they can take command of a situation if need be. We were engaged by the Institute to do the best we could with the Cadets enrolled here and that is exactly what I propose to do. I will be fair but will not brook any nonsense, folly or insubordination either in the classroom or on the drillfield. Cadets will attend classes on a timely basis, prepared daily for the stipulated lesson. Any infractions of regulations will be cause for being placed on report or listed on the demerit roster. I propose to make officers of these men in a manner befitting the dignity, honor and respect that anyone can attribute to any well trained soldier who bases his claim to command on his conduct and ability to lead and function under the most adverse conditions. As my aide in the field, I shall expect you to follow out the principles which I have just explained.

"Should any of the men fail to carry out orders which I shall issue through you, in marching, drill or artillery practice, you will promptly put them on report.

"These measures and procedures may, at first, appear harsh, but I assure you, Caleb, when the men realize why I insist on such rigorous practices, they will, in time, see the propriety of my actions and will acquiesce in everything I advocate."

"I see, sir, I will carry out your orders, just as I have in years past." With that I left him and went back to my quarters.

I had a certain sense of hope that these things would work out as the

Major planned but knowing these youngsters as I did, it appeared that as a Professor, Jackson, would have a harder time than the Major Jackson I had known on the battlefield. He would not have easy going in any of the programs he taught at the Institute. He was up again a group of young men who were accustomed to having their own way at home as well as V.M.I. If Jackson insisted on his program, clashes would occur between teacher and student and no one could accurately foretell how far the Major would go in exercising his authority.

It soon became obvious to me that the gauntlet had been thrown down by the Professor and the students. They may not have taken him seriously at first but now a different tune was being played. he was just as stern and hard bitten on the training ground as he was in the classroom. Many a group was marched and drilled until exhaustion claimed the weakest member. The cadets were too proud to admit any physical weakness and when Jackson ordered a drill or march, they cheered each other with encouragement not to drop in the presence of their drill master thus losing face with their colleagues. This severe and difficult mode of training brought many under-the-breath curses on the head and physical parts of Major Jackson. He was no fool and from time to time, he heard the men cursing at him, but since no one was stupid enough to utter a curse out loud, he pretended not to hear them so he would not be tempted to cite the cadet for disrespect and cursing his superior officer. He knew he was disliked but he was determined to train these young men to a point of excellence.

It was difficult for Jackson to understand why the cadets could not accept him or understand what he was trying to do for them. He was giving them the benefit of his own experiences in military training. He never envied them their wealth, good manners, dress or station in life. His was a background of hard work and sacrifice and his Heavenly Father had long ago advised him in his deep moments of prayer, that predestination was not his sole and singular possession. In the deep convictions of his soul he prayed for the success of every cadet under his instruction. If the Corps only realized how sincere and honest Jackson was about their succeeding, they would have cheered rather than jeered him.

A time came when the Institute was rocked with an incident involving James Walker, a cadet, and Jackson who was his professor. Big Jim, as they called Walker, was accused of precipitating a disturbance. Walked insisted he was not to blame and a shouting match ensued. The Major reminded Walker what the regulations called for and warned him that continuation of his actions would call for the punishment set forth by the code. Walker disregarded Jackson's warning and continued to shout to a point where

Jackson ordered him to leave the room. Walker was forced to leave but not before shouting that he would not apologize or offer regrets for his uncontrolled ranting and accusations against the Major. Jackson charged Walker with code violations which required him to be confined to quarters. When Walker sent a letter to the Administration protesting his treatment by Jackson, he became subject to Court Martial.

Jackson was an old, experienced hand at Courts Martials, having participated in a number of them when he served as a Court member during his tenure in the United States Army. This was an unfortunate incident but Jackson did not deviate from his original method of discipline so he prepared for the trial.

The Court Martial began on May 2, 1852, where Major J. T. L. Preston, served as Court president, Cadet Lieutenant M. P. Christian, served as Judge Advocate and Major William Gilham was the third member of the judicial panel. They listened to the three charges against Walker. The first concerned his refusal to stop talking in Major Jackson's classroom; the second concerned the disrespectful tone of the written excuse to the administration and the third dealt with the illegal act of writing the excuse to the administration. Walker pleaded guilty to the first charge but to an associated fourth specification of disrespectful conduct toward a superior, he pleaded not guilty.

Jackson, who ordered the trial, was the principal prosecution witness. He testified first and related the events in fair detail. He stated that at the end of class, Walker said that his conduct or Jackson's must change and he wanted to talk about it further. Jackson said he refused and requested decent behavior of Walker.

Jackson's testimony continued when he told that things heated up the next morning when he asked Walker to demonstrate the solution to a problem that several of the cadets had done at the blackboard. Walker replied that he did not know how to reach a solution. Jackson pointed out that he had explained the problem the previous day and Walker answered by saying that Jackson had not been clear in his explanation to the class. Another argument ensued and Jackson ordered him to stop yelling. Walker refused and then said he would not stop unless the Major did likewise. Jackson told the court he ordered the cadet to be quiet and Walker continued talking. He then ordered the cadet to take a seat and behave himself. Walker ignored the order. Having no other choice, Jackson ordered Walker confined to quarters. He concluded his testimony by saying that he gave the class sufficient opportunities to ask questions dealing with problems discussed and Walker had no valid reason that could justify his disrespect toward a superior or any excuse for his bad conduct.

Walker decided to conduct his own defense. His strategy was to prove the professor guilty of prejudice against him. If he could prove such a startegem, the tables would be turned on the Major thus nullifying the charges of disrespect against him.

The matter of the written note to the administration was impossible to avoid since the regulations definitely were spelled out governing the situation. Walker therefore, decided to call several of his classmates who were present at the events thinking he could convince the court that there was a conflict between Jackson's testimony and that of his fellow cadets and such a tactic would possibly counter the charge of disrespect. As it turned out, the testimony of the defense witnesses conflicted with Major Jackson's testimony and the court had to decide who was telling the truth.

In order to bolster his defense, Walker had to prove that Major Jackson badgered him. He called on several more classmates to testify and they told the court Walker was respectful and correct in not yielding. They said he was eager to get along with the professor and further stated that the professor lost his temper on at least one occasion and ordered a halt to their conversation.

The following day, Walker, speaking in his own defense and trying to prove Jackson's weaknesses, stated that the professor was rigid, suspicious by nature, irritable, demeaning and argumentative. He had misconstrued Walker's intentions and conduct. He added that it was the Major's word against the cadet and the Major's conduct that rebutted charges of improper behavior toward a professor and superior officer. He claimed the teacher's replies demonstrated treatment which differed from that offered other cadets and he had no other choice but to defend his position and integrity since he believed that the orders to desist were illegal and hence not to be obeyed. Regarding the charge of the excuse as wrong, Walker claimed it was warranted in light of unfair treatment since a gentleman had to defend himself.

The court found Walker guilty of disrespect toward a superior officer. He was found not guilty on the written excuse charge. He had failed to prove his contentions and was dismissed from V.M.I. The court did give him the privilege of resigning if he chose to do so and the Superintendent Francis H. Smith offered him the right of appeal to the Board of Visitors. Walker refused the offer in terms which were disrespectful and insulting to the Superintendent.

The testimony revealed an ''impatient'' Professor and a headstrong cadet. Similar behavior might have passed in a civilian school, but not in a military school such as V.M.I. The court's verdict, however, did agree with Walker and the cadets, that Jackson's behavior as a classroom professor should manifest better comportment than he did. Had Walker controlled his impatience and swallowed his pride, events might not have reached the court martial stage.

Walker wanted revenge. He was incensed with the court's verdict and his dismissal from the Institute. He felt humiliated and wondered how he could face his family and friends back home. He believed Jackson was to blame and the honorable thing to do was to challenge him to a duel. Superintendent Smith heard of the challenge and wrote to Walker's father advising him to come to V.M.I. and take his son home as soon as possible.

Jackson had no physical fear of Walker, having survived combat in the war and relied on his Heavenly Father for protection. He feared no man. He realized Walker was hot tempered and had a restraining order issued by a Magistrate so that legally speaking, he would be protected against any bodily harm. After this was done, Jackson continued his normal routine as if nothing was amiss. He was seen going about Lexington without making any special effort to avoid Walker.

Walker left V.M.I. without ever crossing Jackson's path again. They never had the duel.

Walker's dream of graduation and entry into West Point with an eventual army career was shattered. He did not sit and brood for long as he sought a position with the Chesapeake and Ohio Railroad as an Engineer in Terrain problems. His training at V.M.I. in Military Engineering gave him the education and expertise needed to master a position of this type and it wasn't long before he began to look forward to a lifetime career of some sort.

Walker decided to explore the possibility of becoming a lawyer. After making necessary inquiries, he was accepted as a beginner in the study of law by John B. Baldwin of Staunton, Virginia. He completed his early legal training and became a student of John R. Minor at the University of Virginia for the remainder of the necessary training. In 1854, he earned his law degree. He married Sarah A. Pogue and established himself as a practicing Attorney.

Major Jackson continued to teach at V.M.I., and the court martial issue became history. The cadets did not particularly like Jackson but they learned to respect him for his uncanny and mysterious ability to teach them what they eventually concluded was the only way to wage war to ultimate victory. Many of them went on to West Point and to army careers and Jackson's mark was being felt through his students long before the Civil War.

Chapter 8

Major Jackson was not content in the Episcopal church. Although baptized, there was something amiss in his faith, as he still believed in preordination, predestination and other doctrines which conflicted with the Episcopal church. His search therefore continued for a faith in which he would be more comfortable.

It was about this time that Jackson became firmly convinced his relationship with God was a deeply religious acceptance of the fact that his Heavenly Father's participation in everything that took place, from day to day, was as it should be. He believed that just as the Divine Spirit had formed the universe and established the arrangement of planets and stars in the heavens, the oceans, mountains and plains, so had this all powerful God determined that every human being set on earth would be given a life to lead in which all events would be predetermined. He believed that, upon death, the recipient of that life would spend eternity in the predetermined manner set forth by his Lord. He had come to believe that in order to spend eternity in the arms of his Lord, one must do good deeds, have unwaivering faith, acceptance of anything that occurred and have blind obedience to the word of God. These, he believed, were the required priorities for entering God's kingdom. Having found his faith in a denomination that suited him, he finally resolved the inner struggle of his religious beliefs and convictions when he joined the Presbyterian Church in Lexington, Virginia, November 22, 1851.

The pastor of the church was W. S. White, D. D., a minister of the gospel who was held in great esteem by the members for reverence and devotion to his congregants. Major Jackson spent a great deal of his time discussing the theological reasons for joining the church. He had done his research work on the church very well so that Pastor White had to call on his considerable knowledge of theology and familiarity with comparable Christian faiths in order to satisfactorily answer Jackson.

Gradually Jackson and Dr. White became staunch friends as the Major attended services on a regular basis. When classes for slaves needed a teacher, he volunteered and became their instructor. His work for the slaves, the poor and the needy did not go unobserved. He did not seek praise or glory for the work he did in the vineyard of the Lord. He personally learned a great deal about the unfortunates who attended the Sunday School classes. The experiences helped form his feelings of sympathy and charity for these creatures of God who were different only because of their color and servitude in a system which was not of their making.

Jackson went about his church duties with zeal. He gained much insight as he worked with the slaves, the deacons and the membership. As was the nature of the man, he gave his all to the Lord. The joy he received from his work in the church, increased as he participated in meetings which often led him to the role of leader. Although he was accustomed to leading a group, through his teaching at V.M.I., he felt a bit uncomfortable as he stood before the membership. His prayers were not presented in the fashion he desired. There were too many pauses of silence and he realized he was not a well trained prayer leader. This led him to a decision to join a debating group in hope of improving his delivery. He must learn to do his work in a smooth manner so he labored over public speaking until he felt he had reached a point where he could face the people with confidence.

It was through the Presbyterian church that he met his future wife. He went to a party one evening where he met Ellie Junkin. She was the daughter of Dr. George Junkin, a Northerner, Presbyterian minister and president of Washington College. Jackson was introduced to her and from the first moment, was quite taken with her appearance.

She was not as striking a looking woman as was Senorita Frederica in Mexico City. She was a rather small person, with light brown hair and fair skin. Her gray eyes and winged eyebrows gave her pretty face an expression Jackson had never seen before. She was dressed in a fashionable gown of heather blue which complimented her figure. Margaret, her older sister, a poet and a constant companion, was at her side and dressed in an identical fashion. She seemed to be a bit shy and was a little prettier than Ellie. The girls were inseparable and seemed to enjoy the same things.

Jackson was now 30 years old and had not really looked at another woman since his ill fated love affair with the Senorita. This time was different. He took notice of Ellie and from that day on, did everything in his power to please her. He soon learned the art of courtship as he talked to her father and asked permission to call on Ellie. This time he would press forward to learn everything he could about this young lady. He wanted her to feel comfortable with him.

Dr. Junkin welcomed Jackson's attention to his youngest daughter. He was impressed with the Major and had long been aware of his famous war record and accomplishments at V.M.I. He thought his Ellie would do well to welcome the attentions of such a fine young man. They continued a courtship all that year and on August 4, 1853, they were married.

Tom and Ellie spent their honeymoon in Canada traveling from New York City to Niagara Falls, into Canada and back through Boston, West Point and back to Lexington. The only thing strange about the trip was that Margaret, Ellie's sister, went on the honeymoon with them. There was never a mention of any discord because of the arrangement. It was probably because Jackson realized how inseparable the girls were and realized that Ellie would be much happier if Margaret was close.

Jackson was so in love with his wife that he wanted to share his joy with friends and relatives. He often wrote to friends saying he was married to an ''intellectual and pure lovely lady. She is a great source of happiness to me.'' He clipped a lock of Ellie's hair to send to Laura just so she could see the color, telling her that his beloved reminded him of her. Their life was a quiet, happy one and of great satisfaction to both sides of the family. They often visited relatives and enjoyed the short trips. Jackson's duties had increased at V.M.I. so he had very little trip time to spare.

By early 1854, Ellie announced she was going to have a child. All the love in Jackson's heart seemed to well up inside as he proudly wrote Laura, ''You must be on the lookout for something in relation to me.'' They made preparations for the baby by preparing a nursery in their new home which the Institute provided for them. Ellie spent hours making the fine batiste baby clothes and knitting warm sacques and bootees. Every stitch was one of love and anticipation. It is said that Jackson was never happier than at that time.

In November of that year, Ellie took a jolting stagecoach ride which shook her up considerably. She returned home and went to bed, going into labor prematurely and having a miscarriage later that evening. The shock was too great for her as she died in childbirth. The baby was stillborn.

Jackson was stricken by the loss of his beloved! His beautiful life was shattered and once again, he was faced with despair. He turned to his religion, working in the Church with renewed vigor. Being close to his Lord was his only sense of hope for sanity. The cadets and their training were his major concern but he moved into other interests such as buying a farm outside the village. He was slow to buy much land in Northern territory for the rumors of an impending war had increased and if a Southerner had land in the North, it might be confiscated. He was once again, holding true to his nature by such long term thinking.

The one thing Major Jackson had wanted to do was to travel through Europe. Every time he had planned such a trip something had come up to stop him. First his illness, then V.M.I., his marriage and Ellie's death. It took him so long to recover from his loss that all thoughts had passed from his mind concerning Europe. But now, he was thinking about the trip once again and very abruptly, he announced that he was asking for a six months leave of absence to make the tour. He had been promised the leave a year before and had not made use of it. With leave granted, he made his plans.

He sailed on the steamship ASIA for Liverpool on July 9th. As usual, in his precise manner, he began a journal on the day he left. After traveling through England and particularly the lake country, he went on to Scotland, enjoying the Highlander's life and customs. The castles of past kings, the abbeys and cathedrals interested him to the point he would linger for days. He often stopped at small out of the way inns and country houses as he walked the countryside. He had read so much about the old country and now he felt he was re-living history as he went through the Scottish mills where they made the cloth and on to the canning factory in Dundee where he watched them make their famous jam and marmalade. The picturesque harbor with the old sailing ships gave him hours of joy as he watched vessels coming in and out.

Germany and Switzerland with its magnificent Alps were a wonder to behold. A few days in a Swiss chalet with a kind innkeeper who catered to his every need, did wonders for his health. Then on to Italy to see the age old sculptures and paintings, the ruins of Rome, Mount Vesuvius and back to France with her crooked cobblestone streets and narrow houses crowded together and touched by second story walkways. He loved the gay music and the little sidewalk cafés where he could go to sip café au láit and watch the people.

He had really intended to use only three months of his leave returning in October but his interest in the Old World had grown to a point where he took his savings, intended for investment in more land, and spent it in travel. He went to Waterloo and traveled over the ground where Napoleon fought his campaigns. This was important to him to walk in the famous Napoleon's footsteps.

As luck would have it, his steamer was delayed. Instead of being impatient or disappointed, he was pleased to be allowed a few more days to explore the country. As a consequence of the trip, he returned to Lexington with renewed spirit and vigor and went back to his classes. The townspeople noticed a distinct difference in the Major's personality. They were pleased that he had brought himself out of such deep grief over Ellie and had managed to accept his plight with a resignation that would sustain him. Again, he had to learn to cope with adversity and conquer it.

Some three years after Ellie's death, Jackson found that his loneliness overwhelmed him. He felt the urge to, once again, assume the position of a normal married man, buy a home and perhaps raise a family. He had been so close to this happiness with Ellie, yet she had gone forever and he must live with the future. He knew he would never forget her, nor would he stop loving her, but life had to go on, so he set about looking for another wife.

The Major had met two girls at the home of his friend D. H. Hill, Eugenia and Mary Anna Morrison from North Carolina, daughters of a Presbyterian minister and college president. He had not forgotten them. After making inquiries, he found that they had moved away from Lexington and gone back to Lincoln County, North Carolina. He sat down and wrote Anna a letter recounting their meeting at Hill's home. He told her of Ellie's death and his subsequent travels through Europe. It was a nice, friendly letter which Anna could see, right off, was an entré into a blossoming friendship.

Anna answered the Major's letter and told him of their life in North Carolina, being careful to fill in the time span with interesting bits of information about the family. Upon receiving Anna's letter, Jackson asked for a short leave and prepared to visit her and the family. Anna was much surprised to look out of the window one day and find Major Jackson walking up the steps to her front door!

A tender and loving courtship ensued with Tom writing letters to Anna which she answered immediately. Tom had made up his mind to marry Anna and move her to Lexington as soon as possible. He formally asked Dr. Morrison for her hand and was given a warm welcome into the family. They made hasty plans for a wedding which was held in the Morrison home in July of 1857. Laura and Uncle Cummins made the trip to North Carolina to attend the wedding.

Anna's wedding present from Tom was a gold watch and a set of seed pearls. He took her on a honeymoon to Richmond, up the East Coast to New York and over to Niagara Falls. When they returned from the honeymoon, Tom took Anna to a hotel and set about the business of looking for a home to buy. He wrote one of his friends to tell him about his lovely wife and made mention of the fact he now had a ''lovely wife capable of making a happy home and the next thing was to give her the opportunity to furnish it.''

Tom and Anna went about Lexington looking for just the right house to buy. Several were available so they took much time deciding which would be most suitable for their needs. It took them a few months to come to a decision.

''Anna, I want you to come with me. You'll need a wrap for these cool fall breezes blowing today.''

''Where are we going Tom?''

''I think I've found just the house for you, my lovely bride!'' he said as he helped her don her coat. She put on her bonnet and with an excited expression on her face, followed him out of the hotel.

''I've asked my friend and aide, Sergeant Sparks, to come with us. We need his opinion. He knows more about the structure of a building than anyone I know.''

They walked out of the hotel and prepared to get in the carriage. I was waiting for them.

''Good morning, Mrs. Jackson. It's nice to see you again.''

''Oh, Sergeant Sparks, Tom has me so excited. He says he has found a house.''

''Yes, ma'am, from what he tells me, it will be just what you're looking for. Let me help you in and we'll drive over to Washington Street.''

I took the reins and drove the carriage toward the other end of town while Major Jackson explained to Anna about the house.

''I went over to the bank this morning and talked to Mr. Wall. He said he knew about a house that was for sale. The family had to leave suddenly. It needs some repairs but we can get it at a good price and fix it up the way we want.''

Anna was beaming as we rounded the curve in the road and drove up to the front of a two story town house. I hitched the horses to the post and we all got out of the carriage. Mr. Wall was waiting for us at the front door.

''Good morning, Mrs. Jackson. Come in and look around. It's a bit cool in here because there's no fire going but I think you'll be alright.''

''Thank you, Mr. Wall. I'll look around while you and Tom go with Sergeant Sparks to look at the foundation.''

Anna went from room to room getting a firm picture of the house. She took note of changes she would like to make while the Major and I walked around making a record of repairs needed. Then they met back inside to discuss their plans.

Tom and Anna decided they wanted the house. They signed the papers and went directly to a carpenter who had been recommended, and asked if they could engage him to make the repairs. He said he could start immediately. From that day on, until they moved in a few months later, it was a busy time for the Jacksons.

The first thing to be done was to find some negro servants to help with moving furniture and cleaning the place. Anna directed their work as they scrubbed and polished the floors, cleaned windows and polished the stove in the kitchen. Tom spent all of his leisure time working around the house. He wanted to make it as comfortable and attractive as possible. Although his tastes were simple, he wanted everything to be in perfect order.

Anna chose their furniture which was simple but good. She had drapes made for the windows and curtains for the bedrooms which were on the second floor. It gave her much pleasure to be fixing up a home of their own and Tom could see how happy she was. He jumped into a new life of domesticity as he cleared a plot of ground behind the house and planted a huge vegetable garden. He alsp put in large crops on the farm he had purchased outside of town, using blacks to assist him.

As the Jacksons settled down, their routine included a set pattern of Bible reading, attending church services and family prayers. He would attend his classes at V.M.I. from eight until eleven, then come home for lunch. The afternoons would be spent working in the fields. Anna would often go with him and rest under the shade of the trees, watching him while he worked. Their evenings were spent with Anna reading to him, or playing the piano for his pleasure.

Another tragedy struck when Anna bore their first child, a daughter whom they named Mary Graham. She lived only a few weeks and died from jaundice in May of 1858. When Anna's grief subsided, he took her on a trip North. They visited in New York and other places of interest then went home to lapse into a period of domestic tranquility.

The next two years were spent with Jackson continuing at V.M.I. as a professor. The Slavery question continued as the main topic of conversation in the nation. America was becoming divided and it appeared that many splinter groups were forming. Some for slavery and some violently against it. The abolitionists began to cause more trouble than any other group. They helped fugitive slaves escape to Canada and organized a league among Negroes for their protection against slave catchers, generally causing upheaval among the slave owners. This is when John Brown, an abolitionist, made his mark on West Virginia history. He was considered an outlaw going from state to state, stirring up trouble. It was known by a few of his friends that

Brown considered an invasion of the South in order to free all of the slaves. He had a lot of support and sympathy from the Northerners. Many helped him although they did not realize he was actually planning an invasion.

Brown met with his outlaw friends and planned to raid the arsenal at Harpers Ferry; then armed with guns and ammunition, he would go about the countryside urging the slaves to rebel and fight. His plan went through and on October 16, 1859, he and 18 of his followers captured the arsenal. They never escaped with the guns or ammunition for the local militia bottled them up and kept them in the Arsenal until the next day when Colonel Robert E. Lee forced the fort open and took Brown and his men to jail. There was a trial and Brown was sentenced to hang. It was interesting to note that Colonel Lee was accompanied by a Lieutenant Jeb Stuart, newly arrived from a Western post.

Tension was high during the trial. The sympathizers became so disruptive, that the surrounding countryside and the people were in danger. Lee knew he must have help to protect the people so he contacted Colonel Smith at V.M.I. and asked for assistance.

Colonel Smith called Jackson in the next day, told him what Lee had said, then directed him to take his cadets to Harpers Ferry to protect the people during the hanging of John Brown. Jackson was elated over this small bit of action. He had followed the trial and sensed there would be trouble. He had agonized over the slaves and had often talked to me about the morality of men enslaving men. His religion and deep convictions about God's will were sometimes in conflict yet he went back to his belief that God must have wanted it this way or he would not have let slavery happen.

Jackson knocked on my door when he returned from Col. Smith's office.

"Sergeant Sparks, we are ordered to Harpers Ferry immediately to maintain calm during the hanging of the abolitionist John Brown. We must notify the cadets and have them ready to move in the morning."

"Yes sir, Major. I'll get busy right away. Good thing you have taught them preparedness. They are going to see how it is to go to war. This will be good experience for them."

I went out and notified the cadets of our new assignment. There was a hustle that afternoon and night as every men prepared for duty at Harpers Ferry.

We were ready to move at the first hint of dawn. We traveled in army style with wagons, arms and ammunition and arrived at the designated spot the next day. We were advised to set up temporary quarters and begin a schedule of patrol around the arsenal. Some were assigned the patrol in the village where wives and children of the men lived.

There was an air of hushed expectation as we walked from house to house. Shopkeepers kept their doors closed and locked. Women were warned to stay off the street and all children were kept inside. There were no loud noises or boisterous cries on the night of December 1st. From time to time, we would see someone running through the deepening shadows only to be swallowed up by the darkness. We knew that many of Brown's sympathizers were there yet it was hard to identify them.

Jackson had been advised that they expected trouble from the strangers who seemed to appear out of nowhere. With the help of the local people, we were able to pick up some of them and put them in jail until the hanging was over, but we knew there were many more out there. Our vigil was constant on that dark, cold night. Jackson walked from tent to tent, checking on the cadets.

The field kitchen had been set up and a temporary mess tent raised. Our supper that night was a quiet and solemn one. We had cadets there who had been born and bred in the North and South. They, too, had become old enough to know about the slavery issue and they realized they were there to maintain order while a man was hanged for treason. The issue, although it was treason for raiding an arsenal in preparation for invasion, was not just an issue for one purpose. It was also the issue of free man against the black slave. Many of the young men found it hard to understand but they knew they were there to follow orders and this is what they would do despite their own convictions.

Jackson was obviously in an emotional upheaval over the tense situation. I could see him sitting at the table, with his brow furrowed and his eyes expressionless in deep thought. I knew he was praying to his Lord for the strength needed to carry out this mission. We had faced situations like this on the battlefield in Mexico but there was something different about this one. We were in our own country and facing battle among our own people. I knew, in my heart, that this was the beginning of a struggle which would not end with the hanging.

The day of December 2nd dawned bright and cold. People began to gather hours before the appointed time and our cadets were put in action early. Their constant search for trouble continued throughout the morning. About noon, they were given the signal to surround the scaffold that had been erected for the hanging.

John Brown was led out to the scaffold and up the steps where he was blindfolded and a rope was hung around his neck. We watched as the minister prayed for his soul...then the signal was given and John Brown hung by his neck until he was dead!

Silence peveraded the area. People marched off the grounds and our cadets were marched back to their quarters.

No discussion, no jubilation, no compromise for the man who had made his mark on history.

I think our cadets grew up that day. They realized the seriousness of the crime and as Major Jackson and I took them back to V.M.I. we noted that they stood a little taller than they had when we left. They had become men who were destined to, some day, lead the country in battle. What an enigmatic situation! Here were young men, primarily of the South, being trained by a brilliant Virginian who had graduated frm West Point and fought heroically and bravely in the Mexican War in the Army of the United States, yet destined one day soon to be fighting for the Confederate States of America against all the power and might of the Federal Union which they were defending at the moment against the likes of John Brown and his ilk!

Chapter 9

The Jacksons' domestic bliss was short lived because of the ominous rumbling of "war talk" which was uppermost in the minds of everyone. The nation was bitterly divided over the slavery issue while all the while the states of the South were talking of secession. Their doctrine included the belief that the national government was a league of sovereign states and if they chose, they could withdraw from the Union. South Carolina was the first to secede.

The election of Abraham Lincoln had brought the slavery issue to a head because he had been elected on his platform of national unity which included freeing the slaves, uniting major economic groups with tariffs for manufacturers and a number of other radical changes. The Southerners knew some of the reforms would be in direct contrast to their states rights and more importantly, they would be forced to free their slaves. Therefore, their protest was a planned secession.

Lincoln was inaugurated in March of 1861 and by that time six other states had seceded. They met in Montgomery, Alabama and established a Southern nation, The Confederate States of America, and elected Jefferson Davis as President and Alexander Stephens as Vice President.

Lincoln retaliated by stating, in his inaugural address that secession was illegal and he would hold Federal possessions in the South. This increased the ire of the Southerners, for one of the Federal installations was Fort Sumter, in the harbor of Charleston, South Carolina. Their first act of protest was to fire on the Fort on April 12th and force the garrison to surrender. By April 15th, Lincoln called for the troops to enforce the nation's laws.

The state of Virginia had been undecided about joining the Confederacy but after Lincoln called for troops, it became apparent that this was an unofficial Declaration of War so they promptly joined the Confederacy. Arkansas, North Carolina and Tennessee followed their lead. The capital was moved to Richmond, Virginia in May as the Southern states prepared for war against the North.

Colonel Robert E. Lee was a respected Officer of the Federal army and Lincoln offered him the command of the North's forces but he resigned immediately saying he could never draw his sword against his native state of Virginia. Jefferson Davis heard of Lee's resignation and offered him command of the Confederate troops, the Eastern Army of Northern Virginia. Lee accepted the post and began planning his campaign.

Major Thomas Jackson was soon to realize that all of the training he had given the cadets at V.M.I. was well spent time and effort for on the morning of April 21st he was ordered to lead a battalion of cadets to Richmond. He was to drill and train the thousands of recruits who were coming in from all parts of the South. Davis had called for 100,000 volunteers but to his surprise about 300,000 had answered his call. None of them knew anything about fighting in a war.

Jackson ordered the cadets to be ready to march at one o'clock and as they prepared to leave, he left them for a few minutes to go home and tell Anna goodbye.

Jackson knelt with Anna as they prayed. They read a passage from the Bible;

"For we know that if our earthly house of this tabernacle be dissolved, we have a building of God, a house not made with hands, eternal in the Heavens."

After that, he rose and kissed his beloved goodbye. Anna's tears streamed down her cheeks as she went to the door to watch Tom walk away. Some few minutes later, the clock in the town hall struck one and she could hear the steady rumble of marching feet as the men made their way to Staunton where they would catch the train to Richmond. She went back into the house which echoed the silence. Just a few short hours ago, there was laughter and joy with the sweet anticipation of more to come. And now, there was fear of what harm might befall Tom!

Major Jackson led his battalion into Richmond where the cadets were sent to various jobs. He was without a command because he did not have a provisional rank in the Confederate Army or the Army of Virginia. He was given little attention. People glanced at this tall, mild mannered man who wore no uniform except that of V.M.I. They assigned him a desk job in the Engineering Corps. He said nothing about it but went straight to work writing letters to some of his friends asking for their help in getting him a better position.

It was not long until Tom wrote Anna;

"Last night Governor Letcher handed me my commision as Colonel of Virginia Volunteers, the post I prefer above all others, and has given me an independent command. Little one, you must not expect to hear from me very often, as I expect to have much more work than I ever had in the same time before!"

Jackson's command turned out to be the post at Harpers Ferry. It was the gateway to the Shenandoah Valley and would be guarded. General Harper was in command there and as soon as Jackson arrived, he realized what had happened. The military affairs were suffering, for General Harper and his staff were dressed in fine uniforms and rode strong horses around the town without much thought to security of the area. There were few of the 1000 men who could even present arms and less officers who could teach them how to do it.

The general and his militia officers became enraged when they found out that Jackson had orders to supersede them. The Confederate government had issued orders to reduce the rank of everyone above a captain and fill their places with seasoned and trained soldiers.

When Jackson took over the command, the men looked at him and wondered why he had been sent to lead them. He was still in his old V.M.I. uniform with his cadet cap pulled down over his eyes. He didn't make speeches and he issued no manifestoes. There were no parades and he never spoke of his plans. He went back to his sparsely furnished headquarters on the second floor of a hotel and began changing things.

The garrison of Harpers Ferry began to see major changes within a week. Men were learning how to drill and how to take commands. Jackson didn't hesitate to give instructions and was patient with the men. They were an intelligent group and learned quickly. He did have a time finding officers, for most of the men were totally ignorant of military tactics. The main problem he had was teaching the men discipline. They were free men who had come from large plantations or farms and had felt they were independent. States Rights was the issue for which they fought and not the slavery issue. In fact, many of the volunteers did not own slaves.

Jackson, now a Colonel, spent much of his time drilling the men, gathering muskets and horses, securing cartridges and enough material for the company. There was so much work and planning to be done and this is where I became Jackson's right hand man again. I had the necessary experience to help him get the supplies needed. We would sit and talk for hours after the men went to sleep, planning our next move. I was on Colonel Jackson's recommendation, made Captain and installed as his aide.

The Union army was gathering strength every day. We knew it would be just a matter of time until we would be in the thick of the fighting. That time came when General Joseph E. Johnston came in and relieved Jackson of his command. All of the State troops were mustered into the Confederate army on June 8th and Jackson was given command of the First Brigade. All of the men were Virginians and the only all Virginia brigade in the Army of the Shenandoah.

Johnston left Jackson and the First Brigade at Harpers Ferry to watch the movements of the Union General Patterson who was moving his way into Virginia and on July 2nd he crossed the Potomac at Williamsport. Jackson led the advance toward Falling Waters as Johnston pushed the main body of his army up to Darksville. When he reached there he sent about 300 men against the head of Patterson's column and engaged in a fierce skirmish.

Lee, a long time friend of Jackson, knew what he could do if he was allowed to lead his men. Although Johnston was in command and under the stern control of General Beauregard, Lee realized he would have to exert an unusual amount of military diplomacy to move Jackson to a higher command where he would do the most good for the troops. Lee knew what a strategist Jackson was. He had seen him in action during the Mexcian War. Now he was determined to move him up but he was faced with Beauregard's ire. Gen. Beauregard was a vain man who thought that every successful move of the troops, every skirmish won, and every retreat of the Yankees was due to his own brilliance. Lee knew the objective would be to diplomatically effect Jackson's transfer and make Beauregard think he had done it. This would take some time and thought.

The opportunity came to Lee after he heard of Jackson's victory at Falling Waters. He notified Beauregard of his intention to give Jackson the commission because he thought the Brigadier General could be of more value to the General. Beauregard was pleased that Lee had made the decision and in his own mind, attributed Jackson's success to his own leadership.

On July 3rd Jackson received the commission of Brigadier General from Geneal Lee. He thought it was not just due to the success at Falling Waters, it was a matter of politics where some of his friends had urged his promotion.

General Beauregard was steadily getting information on Patterson's movements from a friend in Washington. She was a lady who kept in touch with important politicans and officers in the Federal command. She worked constantly to secure information for Gen. Beauregard by a series of coded messages and day by day, hour by hour, she would pass vital information on. She played a great part in the success of the Confederate movements and their battles against the North.

On July 16th a man appeared at her house with a message. It was only two words, "Trust Bearer," and with that she wrote out a coded message and gave it to the man; "Orders issued for McDowell to march upon Manassas tonight." He took her message and drove off down the East bank of the Potomac River where he met and gave the message to a waiting cavalryman, who took it to Beauregard at nine that night. The General sent out his orders to his men to fall back from a point close to the Fairfax Court House and proceed to the line of Bull Run. Then he wired President Davis to send the army of the Shenandoah to his support. Davis waited fifteen hours to order General Johnston to support Beauregard. This could have been devastating if McDowell had been organized. However, Johnston's troops marched south from Winchester at dawn with Jackson's brigade taking the lead. The men thought they were retreating and marching towards Massanutten to the right, up the Valley Turnpike.

Suddenly the column was halted and a message was read. A general order;

"Our gallant army under General Beauregard is now attacked by over-whelming numbers. The General Commanding hopes that his troops will step out like men and make a forced march to save the country." With that the column turned east towards Ashby's Gap.

The Confederates marched all of that hot July day. Some shouted and some sang. People ran out along the road and cheered them, bringing buckets of water and baskets of food. The women wept and the young girls waved. General Jackson rode at the head of his brigade on his little sorrel horse.

The Federal army had many adventurers tagging along. They had come to watch the battle between McDowell and Beauregard, but little did they know that a friend of General Jackson, Colonel J. E. B. Stuart of the Confederate Calvalry had fooled Patterson for three days by riding up and telling him that Johnston's troops were not coming to the defense of Beauregard. McDowell relaxed and decided he couldn't send a raw army into a frontal attack across a deep creek where the Confederates held every ford of Bull Run on a line eight miles long. He would wait a few days.

Johnston's troops marched all day July 18th until they came to the Shenandoah where they waded in the water, up to their armpits and across to Ashby's Gap. Another hour took them into Eastern Virginia. They were now twenty miles away from Bull Run mountain and on the other side, lay their comrades who were to confront McDowell and his troops. They were afraid they were almost too late.

The First Brigade halted at a little village called Paris. They were exhausted and hungry and could go no further. Some fell asleep by the side of the road. Jackson realized how tired they were so he never ordered a sentry, he guarded the camp himself.

The sun rose clear in the sky as the First Brigade took the lead again the next morning. The road was ablaze wth shining rifles as the long column of men marched toward Bull Run. Colonel J. E. B. Stuart rode by at the head of his Cavalry regiment. He smiled and waved his hat. It was a fawn colored, broad rimmed hat with a dark brown ostrich plume dangling from the left side. His coat was gray trimmed with white serge collar and cuffs. The sleeves were trimmed with gold braid. His riding gauntlets were of pure white and he made quite a picture as he pranced along on his spirited horse.

Stuart rode along the column yelling greetings to those he recognized. When he smiled, his eyes lit up and his skin glowed soft and pink. He was a daring and careless soldier who feared no one. He loved God and was pious, tried to follow His teachings as did his friend Jackson. They stopped to greet each other during the long march and it seemed as if each gave the other strength to carry on.

The soldiers trudged on until eight that morning when they stopped at Piedmont Station on the Manassas Gap Railroad. There they climbed into the empty box cars and let their legs dangle over the side. People came by and gave them baskets of food and jars of milk. Some negro women came by with trays of fried chicken. The hungry men ate the food and prepared for the long ride to Manassas Junction while the artillery, cavalry and ammunition and supply wagons kept up the march by road.

By four o'clock the Army of the Shenandoah arrived and marched North on the road to Mitchell's Ford about four miles away. General Beauregard was relieved to see his reinforcements and with this help he took nearly eight thousand men with the three brigades and placed them on the Bull Run reserve. Just before the battle, on 20th of July, 1861, the Confederates had 29,000 men of all arms to meet the attack of some 34,000 plus enemy troops.

Beauregard's mystery lady in Washington had been busy. She had received some vital information about McDowell that could change the course of the attack. She hastily dispatched Beauregard another coded message by courier, which was taken to one of his scouts. Shortly after midnight, Beauregard decided to take the offensive himself. The message had been that McDowell was deploying his forces on the Warrenton Turnpike. That meant the Yankees were going to make their attack by passing the Stone Bridge area. This changed Beauregard's strategy and not a moment too soon!

He issued orders for the men to attack at four-thirty A.M. There were to be two brigades to hold the Yankees in check at Stone Bridge while Beauregard's main forces would march as quickly as they could, towards Centerville. They would destroy McDowell's base and he would not be able to communicate with Washington. Jackson's brigade was ordered to go along behind the others and reinforce the troops. By this time it was eight o'clock on the morning of July 21st. There was a short skirmish going on but the assault Beauregard expected had not come. They waited until they could stand it no longer then he ordered the men to advance. Jackson and his men were stationed just inside a thicket of pines when they heard the Yankees coming.

General Bee rode by shouting to Jackson that the Yankees had them far outnumbered. As usual, Jackson showed no alarm as General Bee's men were running in all directions and obviously in a state of panic.

Jackson made the statement to me and to General Bee,

"If we can't beat them then we will face them head on and give them the bayonet."

General Bee watched Jackson's men as they stood quietly waiting for the attack.

"Look, there is Jackson, standing like a stone wall. Rally behind the Virginians!"

Those words will live in history for that is when General Jackson was given the name of Stonewall! It followed him the rest of his days.

The fierce battle with McDowell's troops ensued until the Rebels chased them back toward Washington. Just as the Federals were retreating down the Henry House Road, President Davis rode up to survey the damage and congratulate the Generals for their fine leadership. Jackson had been nicked in the hand by a shell so he went to Major McGuire, a doctor, to dress his wound. He was still excited over the battle. Jerking his head, with eyes still blazing, he told the doctor,

"Give me 10,000 men and I will be in Washington tomorrow morning."

We realized it was possible for Jackson to do just that but I knew Beauregard well and he thought he had won the battle so there was no chance of Jackson getting such a command. The request would never be made. Jackson could have won the war, but there was always "if."

The men celebrated that night. Victory over the Yankees was sweet! Jackson's brigade had lost heavily as 561 of his men had been either killed or wounded. He led his men to a camp south of Mitchell's Ford where they stopped for a well earned rest.

Jackson got up at sunrise and before he had breakfast, he stopped to write his pastor in Lexington. The letter said,

"In my tent last night, after a fatiguing day's service, I remembered that I had failed to send you my contribution to our colored Sunday School. Enclosed, you will find my check for that object, which please acknowledge at your earliest convenience and oblige."

Yours faithfull,

T. J. Jackson

By the time Jackson's letter reached the pastor, he had already heard the news of Jackson's superb and strategic performance at the battle of Manassas yet there was no word of it in the letter—only his concern for the negro slaves he taught each Sunday. The good pastor told his friends about the letter and remarked that it was just like Jackson not to reveal military information or to brag about his accomplishments.

The talk of the nation was that Washington was going to be captured by the Confederates. Just when and how was the question. Federal troops had gone behind the lines to plan their defense. Their stocks were low and they needed extra time to gather their supplies and ammunition. Meanwhile, the Confederate armies were doing the same. It seemed the whole world waited for another move to be made, but neither side was anxious to be first!

Jackson kept his men in a state of readiness. He saw that enough arms and ammunition were supplied so that the men could be called into service at a moment's notice. Jackson knew the value of being ready for an attack so he never relaxed nor did he let his men become complacent. They spent the summer drilling. Many, however, came down with dysentery and thousands were sent home on furloughs. North and South learned quickly that war was deadly!

President Davis was swept into the thick of a political frenzy. He didn't want to capture Washington but his Generals did, for they could see that General McClellan was organizing at his own leisure and would be able to come at them, with an overwhelming force, march in and out, crushing the Confederates. But Davis had another idea. He thought, if the Confederate armies could remain on the defensive, France and England would come to their aid, and the war could be ended without more bloodshed. The Generals disagreed with him but were unable to change his mind.

Jackson had another plan in mind but had not been able to advise the Commanding General, due to his subordinate rank. This was about to change for he had just been promoted to Major General and with this rank, he might be able to exert more influence. With this in mind, he went to see General Gustavus Smith.

The General was sick at the time but urged Jackson to sit down and talk with him. Jackson did and proceeded to tell him what he thought should be done. He told Smith he thought McClellan would not try to fight that fall and if the Confederate troops remained inactive McClellan's troops would have had time to train more recruits and become better organized. Besides, the Federal troops outnumbered the Confederates about three to one. He added, "if the President would reinforce this army by taking troops from areas not threatened and move them into this area, we could invade before winter sets in."

Smith listened attentively to Jackson's plan.

"We could cross the upper Potomac and take Baltimore which would give us possession of Maryland then we could cut off entry and exit from Washington, force the Union Government to leave the capital and beat McClellan's army, if they came out in the open, and then live on the country we would have taken. We would make the North understand what it would cost them to hold the South at bayonet's point."

Smith looked at Jackson and shook his head. It was no use and he knew it for he understood how President Davis felt. He told Jackson about the conference Davis had with his generals when they urged him to invade and how he turned them down.

Jackson rose, shook hands with Smith and thanked him for listening then got on his horse and rode off. He knew that unless he had greater power he could do nothing more. He prayed that God would see fit to give him that power soon.

On October 26th, Major General Jackson assumed command of the troops in the Shenandoah Valley, with headquarters located at Winchester. He looked at his new orders and turned to his friend, Dr. White who was visiting him,

"Had this communication not come as an order, I should instantly have declined it, and continued in command of my brave old brigade."

Jackson hated to leave his men. He had worked with and trained them to be fine soldiers and now he would have to leave them behind. Also, he would still be subordinate to Johnston. These men were the cream of Virginia, and as he looked at them, with their coat collars adorned with gold bars and the bright red sashes around their waists, he thought of the struggle they had, to become such fine soldiers of the famous Stonewall Brigade. He knew he had to tell them he was leaving and somehow, he had to instill in them, for the last time, their sense of pride and zest for victory of this struggle between the Army of the Potomac and the Army of the Shenandoah!

By the first week in November, the now famous Major General Stonewall Jackson was ready to leave and take over the forces of the Army of the Shenandoah. There was one last farewell to be made which he dreaded. He called out his brigade, mounted "Old Sorrel" and rode to the front of the line.

"I am not here to make a speech, but simply to say farewell. Throughout the broad extent of country through which you have marched, by your respect for the rights and property of citizens, you have shown that you are soldiers not only to defend, but able and willing both to defend and protect. You have already won a brilliant reputation throughout the army of the whole Confederacy; and I trust, in the future, by your deeds in the field, and by the assistance of the same kind Providence who has hitherto favored our cause, you will win more victories and add lustre to the reputation you now enjoy. You have already gained a proud position in the future history of this, our second War of Independence. I shall look with anxiety to your future movements and I trust whenever I shall hear of the First Brigade on the field of battle, it will be of still nobler deeds achieved, and higher reputation won!"

He then stood up in his stirrups, raised his voice and said,

"In the Army of the Shenandoah, you were the First Brigade. In the Army of the Potomac, you were the First Brigade. In the Second Corps of the Army you are the First Brigade. You are the First Brigade in the affections of your General, and I hope by your future deeds and bearing you will be handed down to posterity as the First Brigade in this our second War of Independence. Farewell."

Chapter 10

General Jackson moved into Winchester to assume command of the Army of the Shenandoah. He was greeted by old friends, politicians and many family members of his Stonewall Brigade. It felt good to be back among those he knew. There was much work to be done and he set about the task of organizing his forces. He found that he had a few undisciplined companies of militia who were completely unorganized. This meant all of his time would be spent in shaping up the forces to defend the extreme left of the Confederate lines.

Jackson was left to defend the left, Beauregard and Holmes would defend the righ and General Daniel Hill would defend the center at Leesburg. He had to be ready to march to Manassas at any given moment. McClellan might decide to attack and it was his duty to observe the movements of the Federal troops and keep in touch with Hill and Beauregard.

With these preliminary plans made, he set about the task of writing Anna at her father's home in North Carolina and telling her they could be together for a while. He directed her to take the first available stage and come to Winchester where he had quarters ready. They were to live at the Presbyterian manse with the family of the minister, Doctor Graham, who had opened up his home to them.

Anna packed her bags and took the first available stage. She was delighted that they would have time together. Her father knew Dr. Graham and felt she would be safe with them should Tom have to be away for any length of time.

The stage made the long, hard trip through a cold rain. The first harsh winds of an oncoming winter blew against the isenglass and Anna felt their chill. She bundled up in the warm wool rug and kept her feet on the heated bricks. The thought of being with her beloved was all she needed to brace her. They made good time all day and as the dusky shadows began to fall, they drove into a little country inn for the night. She and her friend, who was also making the trip to be with her husband in Winchester, went into the cozy room and asked for their reservations.

A nice warm supper and a room which was heated by a bright fire helped to relax the ladies as they prepared for bed. Anna was glad she had someone to talk to.

"Just image Jane, tomorrow night we'll be with our husbands."

"Oh yes, and what a joy. I haven't seen Jim in a year. How long has it been since you've seen Tom?"

"Not since he said goodbye in Lexington, over a year ago. It's been hard to be separated from him."

"Let's get some rest now. I'm so excited over tomorrow, I doubt if I can sleep, but I'll try."

Jane reached over and blew out the lamp. The warm down covers were comforting as she and Anna felt the fatigue of the day slipping away. They listened to the rain as it blew against the window panes and soon they drifted off to sleep.

The stage pulled up in front of the Taylor Hotel in Winchester. Anna looked about for Tom but all she saw was a group of soldiers. Then one of them came out of the crowd and walked toward her.

"Tom?"

"Yes, my dearest esposa. Welcome!" he said as he threw his arms around her and they kissed.

"I am so glad to see you, my dearest. I hope we shall never be separated again for so long!"

"Well, my love, we will be together now, for a while at least. Come, let me take you to your new home!"

They went down the street while I followed behind carrying Anna's bags and Jim, Tom's trusted servant who had not left his side since Lexington, followed us with more bags.

Anna turned around to direct her words to me.

"Captain Sparks, I am so glad to see you. I have felt better ever since I found out you were with my husband again. I know what the two of you can do together." Then she turned to Jim;

"Jim, the General writes me that you are doing a fine job of taking care of him. How do you manage to find his food when you're out there in the field?"

"Miz Anna, it sho is hard sometimes, but the folks have been good to us. They bring us de General's buttermilk and I makes him cornbread at the mess tent. I sees to it dat he gets some fruit. We stop and git apples and berries from de farmers. Sometimes we find grapes and pears. De General, he ain't 'fraid to ask em for things. I tries to keep up with him, and keep his clothes washed as bes' I can!"

"Oh, Jim, you are such a faithful helper, and I thank you for all you are doing," Anna said as they walked up to the entrance of the manse.

Dr. Graham and his wife met them at the door, giving them a friendly welcome. You would have thought we were members of the family the way they treated us. We were shown to our rooms. A large room for Tom and Anna, a smaller room for me and Jim was taken to the servants' quarters to his room. We didn't feel so bad about moving in with the Grahams when we saw what a big house they had.

Anna busied herself with unpacking and arranging her things in their room, then went downstairs to help Mrs. Graham with the house. Although there were servants, there was still plenty to do, for people from the church were coming and going. They had a room set up for volunteer war workers who rolled bandages, filled first aid kits and knitted socks and scarves for the soldiers.

Tom spent his free hours talking to Dr. Graham. They engaged in heated discussions about doctrine of the various religions. There was little time for relaxation, much less the time needed to work with the church. But he was glad for the opportunity to become a part of the community and attend church among those he loved.

The good news came to General Jackson one day when he received notice that Johnston had decided to reinforce him with his old Stonewall Brigade. They were on their way and would arrive in two days. The General called me in.

"Sparks, good news! The Stonewall Brigade is on its way to reinforce us. They'll be here in two days."

"Good, sir. We need those men and I know they are happy to be under your command again. Just hasn't been the same without them."

"Yes, I need them. This will give us about 4,000 more men. Go see about quarters for them. You take charge and when they arrive, let me know."

I left Jackson and went to prepare for the men. There was much work to be done in so short a time but since I was entrusted with their presence I didn't mind at all.

With the Stonewall Brigade in place, Jackson turned his thoughts to military strategy. The Federals had gathered strength and just 35 miles away in the village of Romney, the Federal General, Kelly, had it covered with 5000 men. Jackson wanted to take Romney back, then invade Pennsylvania and Pittsburgh, and go on to Baltimore and Washington. He realized how President Davis felt about taking such a risk so he decided to just ask for reinforcements.

President Davis sent him General Loring's idle division of 7000 men. When they arrived, Jackson was surprised to find that they were little more than civilians who knew nothing of fighting a war. It was New Year's Day and his plans were made for fighting despite the poor quality of Loring's troops.

They marched along and like raw recruits the men discarded their blankets and coats because the weather was mild, but by January 5th the weather changed and they found themselves in the middle of a storm with sleet and snow coming down. The temperature had dropped to zero.

Loring's men complained of the terrible treatment. Jackson heard them but never commented or acted as if he was going to change their direction. They grumbled about their "terrible conditions" and when Jackson took a brigade off and left them at an outpost, they registered a formal complaint to the Secretary of War requesting a change to some other place.

When Jackson returned and found what they had done, he was enraged. All of his work was undone by their untimely action, not to mention the disgrace of the forces requesting a transfer. He promptly sat down and wrote the Secretary of War and resigned, requesting that he be ordered to report for duty to the Superintendent of the Virginia Military Institute at Lexington. He added that if the War Department honored the protest of Loring's men because they did not like their conditions, then the next protest might be sent to Johnston and Lee. He would not accept this meddling in military affairs.

His resignation was not accepted so he settled down to a life of drilling the troops and preparing them for future battles. His main objective was to gather information. This was done by setting up a network of spies. He had them spotted around the countryside with each one bringing him information vital to the movement of the Federal troops. Some were businessmen, one was a politician, another a farmer near the Union line and a beautiful young woman named Neda of Pennsylvania Dutch descent who lived just over the Union lines. She became friendly with some of the Southern families while on a visit to Virginia. When the war started, she became a Southern sympathizer and helped them in many ways.

Jackson called Jeb Stuart in one day to talk with him about Neda.

"Jeb, you are the most dashing soldier I know and I have a job for you. It will be done in the utmost secrecy and you are the only one I know whom I can trust."

"What is it General? What can I do?"

"There's a young woman named Neda who lives just over the Union line. She is one of my spies and is very valuable to our cause. She has become friends with the Union General and in conversations with him, he tells her many of their plans. Also, she has access to the stores of ammunition and their drugs. We need all of these things. I want you to meet Neda tomorrow night just over the hill outside of her village. The two of you will make arrangements for future meetings and transfer of ammunition and drugs. You realize this is a dangerous assignment so you are free to turn it down."

Jeb's eyes were gleaming with excitement.

"General, this will be a pleasure. I'll meet Neda tomorrow night. Just give me some identification."

Jackson quickly wrote out a note and handed it to Jeb.

"Leave here in plenty of time to meet Neda at midnight. She will be waiting for you in a little house by the river. Be careful!"

Colonel Stuart carefully dressed for his mission. This time he was not in his gleaming uniform, but in a dark coat and trousers. He waited until night to go out and get on his horse, being careful to avoid anyone who might be watching. The troops had retired to their tents and the sentry was at the other end of the field when Jeb rode off. He pulled his cap down over his forehead and slung a blanket over the horse so that they would become as invisible as possible as they rode through the darkness.

Jeb followed the trail to the river. There was not a soul in view and only the sound of some wild animal slinking through the woods now and then. He took out his pocket watch and struck a match to see the time. 11:30 and so far so good he thought as he made his way toward the bridge. Then he spied the house with a faint light flickering inside. He approached with caution as he heard the front door squeak and a figure stepped out.

"Hello, anyone there?"

"Yes, is that you Colonel?"

Jeb hitched his horse to a tree limb and walked toward the door. There in the flickering light stood the most beautiful woman he had ever seen. She had silvery blond hair which hung in ringlets down to her shoulders. Slight of figure with a dark dress and shawl covering her shoulders. She extended her hand to Jeb.

"Come in, Colonel. Are you sure no one followed you?"

"Yes, ma'am. I was careful. General Jackson said you would be waiting.

Aren't you scared to come out here?''

"No, I have those around me, who are sympathizers and protectors. They are watching the Bluecoats while we talk!''

Jeb sat down at a table while Neda told him about the plan she had to get ammunition and drugs to the Confederate troops. She had managed to get the supplies and had them stored in a barn not too far from the river. He was to bring a wagon and two of his trusted soldiers to the bridge the next night. She would be there to meet him and they would transfer the supplies. With this arranged she and Stuart sat and talked while she made coffee for him and served some of her apple cake which she had brought along.

Jeb watched Neda's face as she talked of the secrets which she managed to drag out of the Union General. She told him of the parties she would attend and pour ale for the General until he was just tipsy enough to talk, then she would lead him on until she got the information. He was fascinated as he listened to her courageous acts to steal their supplies and store them for transfer. She had helped many of the soldiers by stealing small amounts of drugs and much needed medicine, then putting them in the secret pockets of her big white apron and walking right across and through Union lines to meet the Southerners on the other side.

They had talked for hours but Jeb knew it would soon be daylight so both of them had to get back while they had the cover of darkness. He donned his cap and she put her shawl around her shoulders, and walked out of the door. A man came up and took her arm.

"Are you alright, Miss Neda?''

"Oh yes, John, I want you to meet Colonel Stuart. You will meet him at the bridge tomorrow night to make the transfer.''

"Good to meet you Colonel. We will be there at midnight. Be sure to bring a cover for your wagon.''

Jeb said goodbye and mounted his horse. Neda and John vanished into the darkness as quietly as they had come. It was getting daylight as Jeb rounded the bend to the camp. The soldiers would be getting up soon so he went straight to Jackson's headquarters to give him the news. After their talk, Jeb went home to his wife.

"Jeb, where have you been? I've been so worried.''

"Had to do some special duty last night, my dear. I'm sorry you worried but I couldn't tell you about it. Now all I need is some sleep for I have to go out again tonight.''

"Come, let me turn down the covers. But first, eat your breakfast. You must be starved.''

He ate a good hot meal and then bid her goodnight as he wearily fell down across the bed. She covered him and tiptoed out of the room for Jeb fell asleep as soon as his head hit the pillow.

The only three men Jackson trusted with his secret was Jeb, Jim, his servant, and me, so the three of us were elected to make the secret run. Old Jim was as excited over the trip as I was. He'd been almost everywhere with Jackson but had never been trusted to do such a job as this. He helped us with the wagon and horses and no one suspected that he was doing anything out of the ordinary. He took them down the road and waited for us to arrive. We started out about 10 p.m. and made our way down the trail.

We met Neda and John at the entrance of the covered bridge. Behind them was a wagon full of ammunition and medicines so sorely needed for our troops. With this we could bring our sick soldiers back to health and use the ammunition to drive back the Union troops. What an act of good fortune this was!

The men unloaded their wagon and transferred the boxes to our wagon. They worked swiftly and silently until the last box had been carefully stored and the wagon covered.

"Thank you, Miss Neda. General Jackson says to tell you that what you are doing for us will long be remembered!"

"Colonel, I have been repaid by what you are doing for the country. I'm just glad I can do this for the Southerners."

With that, we bid the men goodbye and Neda said,

"I'll let you know when I have another wagon load. We'll meet at the same place provided the Yankees haven't taken this side of the river."

We drove back and unloaded the stores in the barn. Jim covered them with hay so no one could tell that there was anything there except feed for the horses.

"Sparks, I want to thank you and Jim for your help. Go get some rest now. Don't tell anyone about our mission."

"Colonel Stuart, you are a fine friend. The General told me he's mighty proud of what you're doing for your country."

Jim had had just about all of the excitement he could stand and while we were talking he slipped off to a corner of the barn and fell asleep on the hay covered floor. Poor tired Jim, I thought. How could we fight this war without him?

McClellan had nearly 200,000 men by February and the future looked extremely dark and very gloomy for the Southern armies. Confederate troops were retreating in every direction. Johnston had 32,000 men and Jackson had 4000 men. They were outnumbered three to one when McClellan decided to invade Virginia. On February 27th General Banks crossed the Potomac at Harpers Ferry, in accordance with the general order of the Union High Command. Johnston asked his men to fall back and conform to the battle plan laid out for them. He expected Jackson to follow but Jackson asked permission to hold his ground. He asked for reinforcements but received none so as Banks, with 38,000 men, advanced on Winchester, Jackson with barely 4,000 men marched north to meet him.

Banks had heard that Jackson's troops had swelled to 11,000 and that his ramparts at Winchester were well fortified, therefore he was cautious in his movements. General Jackson had planned a night attack against Banks but through a slip of orders, his men had been sent 12 miles away and there would not be enough time to get them back. As a result, he had to order his men to retreat. The army had to camp at Mount Jackson which was twenty-five miles above Strasburg. There they waited for Banks to make the next move.

Colonel Turner Ashby, a member of the Cavalry, became one of Jackson's indispensable men. He kept Jackson informed about the Federal movements. One day he came in to tell the General that the Yankees were retreating. McClellan was going to move his large army by water to Fort Monroe and then he was going to go overland towards Richmond and capture the city.

Jackson led some 2000 Confederate infantry into the Valley Pike and engaged in a bloody battle at Kernstown with Shields' men. Ashby's Cavalry came to the General's assistance and held the Yankees off until Jackson's men could retreat. They had been overpowered by the Union forces and suffered their first setback since the War started. Jackson had been whipped on the field which he yielded to the enemy. There was one good thing to come out of this disaster; Shields had been badly shaken by Jackson's troops so he didn't try to follow them. He thought Jackson had reinforcements close by so they retreated from the area.

Most Southerners thought Jackson's setback at Kernstown was a disaster. They compared it to Fort Donelson and Fort Henry. Banks had telegraphed Lincoln that Jackson's 15,000 men had been smashed and virtually decimated as they fled in confused rout from the battle. This pleased Jackson when he heard the news. He knew that his spies had been at work and had passed on the misinformation to Banks. The plan worked, for Banks lay idle and didn't move his troops anywhere for a whole week.

To General Stonewall Jackson, the setback at Kernstown was a victory of sorts. He knew he had bluffed Banks and Shields and that is exactly what he wanted to do. His watchword was to deceive and mystify the enemy and put his faith in God rather than in numbers that might or might not be correct.

Banks had written Washington that he intended to strike Jackson immediately. Again, he moved not another inch until April 17th and then Jackson held the line from New Market to Luray. Banks was stopped once more. His troops had time to rest and enjoy their free time but Jackson was alert to all changes of the Federal's strategy.

Banks began to move forward capturing the town of New Market which meant Jackson's men had to retreat. He knew if he fell back towards Staunton, Banks' 20,000 men could overcome him. Jackson said not a word about the dilemma for he had another plan in mind. A few days later he received a letter from General Robert E. Lee, who had been put in Chief command of all military operations. He suggested that Jackson take General Ewell's division and attack Banks in an effort to drive him back from Fredericksburg. Jackson was delighted for this suggestion was the very one he planned to make. Now Lee had solved his problem. He would take Ewell's division and attack Banks!

On April 30th Jackson initiated his first bold stroke. General Ewell came over the Blue Ridge of Swift Run Gap and occupied Elk Run Valley while Jackson took his men to Port Republic, and on to Gordonsville where they boarded long lines of freight and cattle cars. They thought they were going eastward to Gordonsville, instead the engines puffed as they started and took the troops back to the Blue Ridge and through Rockfish Gap to Staunton.

The Yankees were expected to arrive in Staunton at any minute and the townspeople were left almost defenseless. Can you imagine how happy they were when they saw our trains steam in? They had protection at last. Their glee did not last long as Jackson took his army and marched west toward the Alleghenies leaving Banks a wide open invitation to take Staunton.

Banks soon heard of Jackson's move and began to wonder what he was doing. It seemed Jackson and his army had been swallowed up by the earth. McDowell marched in vain for Jackson until he heard that he had returned to the Valley and had reached Mount Solon a few miles south of Harrisonburg.

McClellan's army had almost pushed on to Richmond and there was great doubt that the Confederate armies could save their capitol. President Davis, anticipating its fall had already ordered the evacuation of all important papers and documents which were housed in the Capitol. It was a dark time for the Southerners. There was one last call from the people to hold Richmond to the last man. No one knew where Jackson was and there was little hope that he could come to their rescue.

But they were wrong because Jackson was ready to move. The Valley army moved north from Mount Solon and Jackson led the march. The arrived at the cross roads which led to eastern Virginia or Front Royal. Leaving Luray behind, they headed down the Valley. Jackson rode in front of the infantry and into the Valley forests. There in the thicket stood a bareheaded girl waiting to talk with Jackson. She called him aside and told him the Yankees were at Front Royal and Strasburg, then told him how many men they had and exactly where they were.

They marched on to the pine woods of Luray Valley just ten miles from Front Royal that night of May 22nd while General Banks who was at Strasburg relaxed his guard and Colonel Kenly and his troops took a long expected breather.

The next morning, on the southern edge of the town, there was the sound of shuffling feet and the Federals saw a long line of Confederate infantry coming at them. The blast of bugles shattered the quiet, and a volley of musket fire came down at them. After the first attack came four others in rapid sequence. The fighting was swift and complete as Kenly was cut down. Only 400 of the 1000 men escaped and their garrison was practically wiped out. Jackson came up and cut off the wires from Front Royal to Washington. Munford's cavalry guarded Manassas Gap to the east while Ashby's men controlled the Strasburg and Staunton roads.

When Kenly's forces straggled in, General Banks had one comment; "I must develop the force of the enemy." Some people in Washington wondered why Banks suddenly made up his mind to retreat. He led his army back to the safety of Winchester.

As Banks' Infantry moved into Winchester, his wagon trains followed slowly behind. Colonel Ashby and his men fell upn them and captured the wagons, teams, kitchens, tents, food, ammunition, nine thousand rifles and many prisoners. Ashby's men were totally undisciplined and Jackson wished they were more controlled but he found Ashby indispensable.

Jackson and his Confederates followed Banks and advanced on Winchester. His men formed a line of battle, yelling as if they were one force. The Yankees broke and ran through the streets with Jackson's men close behind. Stonewall Jackson galloped by, screaming at his men,

"Press forward to the Potomac! Forward to the Potomac!"

He had counted on Ashby and his men, and G. H. Steuart who commanded Ewell's cavalry to reinforce his ranks, but neither appeared so Banks escaped and by noon of the next day he crossed the Potomac at Williamsport.

The newspapers carried, in the Sunday edition, the news that Banks was defeated and the enemy was about to take Washington.

Stanton wrote to Lincoln, "There is no doubt that the enemy in great force, is marching to Washington." As a result, the governors of all the Northern States were called upon to send as many men as they could muster together with equipment, supplies, guns and ammunition to assist in repulsing any attack on the Capitol City.

The Northern states were in a panic. Most of the military believed Jackson's forces had reached some 30,000 to 60,000 men. Lincoln was so disturbed by this that he dismissed any thought of McClellan moving against Richmond and ordered McDowell to remain in place until further notice. Lincoln thought only of crushing Jackson so he ordered Fremont to close in on the rear of Jackson's troops and cut off his retreat. They were planning to surround Jackson and his 17,000 men with 35,000 of the Federals.

We began the march back to Winchester on the 29th. When we arrived we heard that Shields had retaken Front Royal. The General sent no reply, just smiled at the courier, bid him goodbye and promptly closed his eyes and went to sleep.

Jackson pressed on toward Strasburg. As he passed over Fishers Hill he saw the Federals closing in. He did not stop or fall back. Instead he kept on going until he reached Woodstock.

In the period from May 19th to June 1st, the Valley Army of 17,000 men had covered one hundred and seventy miles, made the enemy retreat, paralyzed the activity of 170,000, captured property worth $300,000, captured 3000 prisoners and 9000 rifles and still managed to move all of their convoy without the loss of a single horse and wagon. Their losses totalled 600 officers and men.

Jackson had pursued the enemy, deceived and tricked them and put the people of thirteen Northern states in a panic. But he was not satisifed with this. He looked toward the enemy, stood up in the middle of the field, raised his right arm while clenching his fist, and shouted:

"I am not through with you yet!"

Chapter 11

In planning his strategy, General Jackson assumed Shields would try to follow him, going by way of the Luray Valley. As a precaution, Jackson sent troops aheads to burn down and destroy the bridges of South Fork which were below the town of Luray. The river could not be forded because of the high flood, thus Shields would be isolated from Fremont.

Shields, however, was still hopeful that he could come behind Jackson and finish him off, but he didn't anticipate the possibility of Ashby's cavalry coming to meet him. On June 6th, Ashby's strongest and most forward lines began to break before the Federal onset. Ashby, riding in front, had his horse shot from under him. He got to his feet and shouted,

"Get up and charge men! For God's sake charge!"

The men charged but Ashby was in the line of fire and was shot through the heart.

Jackson felt the loss of this great cavalry commander and sent a note to one of the other officers in Ashby's command;

"Poor Ashby is dead. He fell gloriously. We can remember him as one of the noblest soldiers in the Confederate army!"

The Stonewall Brigade camped in the village of Port Republic. Major Imboden knew this and wanted to talk with the General. He set out on his horse to find us. The whole camp was buzzing with activity as Imboden rode up to a house which was supposed to be Jackson's temporary quarters.

"Come in, Major. Glad to see you," Jackson said.

"I hope I haven't disturbed you so early in the morning but I need to discuss something."

Jim brought them coffee and some of his biscuits. The aroma of frying food drifted through the kitchen and Jim said,

"Mas, Tom, you and da Major jes be content with dis coffee for a while til I gits de breakfast ready, den I'll call you to de table."

"Thank you Jim," he said as he turned to the Major and commented,

"You see, you're invited to breakfast. Jim cooks the best ham and eggs in the camp."

"I'll look forward to it, General. In the meantime I want to offer my congratulations on the magnificent results of your four week campaign against our enemy, the Union armies.

"Yes, God blessed our army again yesterday and I hope, with His protection and blessing today will still be better."

They spent an hour talking about current plans for an attack on the nearby Lewis farm and their future plans for another skirmish. By the time they had finished breakfast, the sun was well over the horizon and it was time to begin fighting again.

The Confederates did do better that day. Jackson advanced the attack under General Charlie Winder, on the Lewis farm and Federal army retreated to the Luray Valley. Fremont began retreating to Harrisonburg and Jackson sent his cavalry, which was now under the command of Colonel Munford, in pursuit of the fleeing enemy. The Union officer thought he was being chased by the main body of the Confederate army and became more bewildered than ever.

On the 12th of the month, Jackson took his army westward to the village of Mount Meridian on the Shenandoah where the tired veterans rested for five days. Jackson took advantage of this idle time to further deceive the enemy. He issued orders that no one could pass the picket line, then he gave a few people false information. Secretly, he planned to elaborate on his operations to beat the Federals. Now that he had the upper hand, he meant to keep it. He also sent out some information, that he intended to clear the Yankees out of the Valley and he might even invade Maryland. This plan was broadcast to the Federals and had the effect Jackson hoped for.

Lee and Jackson were about to deliver the great counter-stroke. On June 17th Lee sent Jackson a letter outlining the whole plan. He intended to gather a great army with Jackson's units being the most important part, then meet to descend on Porter's exposed troops. Lee would back up Jackson with divisions of General Lawton and General Whiting followed close behind.

Trains were readied for the men to board in Richmond and the secret was an open one. Federal prisoners of war who marched by were able to count the regiments. The truth was that no one except Lee, Jackson and

Portrait of "Stonewall" Jackson by Routzan (1862)

Munford knew Jackson's real strategy. The Federals were still asking questions, "Where is Jackson?" He could appear almost anywhere. They still thought he was in his front above Strasburg.

The Valley army was now in eastern Virginia and they demanded to be told their destination. They got their answer from the pastor of the Gordonsville Presbyterian Church. He told them they were to march to Culpeper Court House to head off a newly created force of the enemy. As they marched, they were told not to answer any questions of civilians. No one dared to breach Jackson's orders, therefore as they walked, and people asked them where they were going, they would just look at them and say nothing.

On June 21st the top leading unit of Jackson's army reached Frederickshall in Louisa County where they stopped for Sunday worship. He had been concerned about their lack of participation in Sunday services and was determined to give them a day to devote to prayer. He thought they needed to get as close to their Lord as possible.

The next morning, Jackson accompanied by his Chief of Staff, Major Robert Lewis Dabney, rode quietly through the pre-dawn darkness towards Richmond. No one knew where they were going and most did not realize they had gone. By Monday noon, they rode through the streets of Richmond and headed toward a remote section of the town. They were on their way to meet General Lee.

They were dusty and bedraggled as they got off their horses and walked into a farmhouse. The first person they saw was General Daniel Hill, then James Longstreet, Ambrose Hill and General Lee.

"Welcome gentlemen," Lee said as they walked in.

He took them down a long hall to a room where a large round table and six chairs had been set up for a meeting. Lee began talking.

"The four of you have been invited to this council of war because you have been selected to deliver a counterstroke against that part of McClellan's army which lies north of the Chickahominy River. I have the Federals exactly where I want them and I want to fall back on the exposed positions of their army."

Jackson was really excited. He knew exactly what Lee was talking about for it was the same plan he had thought out and delighted in the fact that his commanding general had the same design for battle as he did.

The generals present were told by Lee that there would be a total force of some 60,000 men. Jackson's command had about 18,000 plus troops and the rest of the fighting sections would come from the remaining generals. The plan was to attack and destroy Porter before McClellan would have a

chance to reinforce him or have any opportunity to withdraw if the fighting
went against the Union army. The ultimate destruction of McClellan's corps
would compel him to retreat to his base of supplies at the White House.
Then, if he could be cut off from his base, he would become demoralized
and his entire army of about 105,000 men could be annihilated.

The five men knew the maneuver would be fraught with danger for
the Confederates but Lee was not afraid and certainly Jackson was not
concerned with any risk involved. He had proven that many times on dangerous and chancy operations. The commanding general was willing to risk
everything on one hard blow and Jackson was willing to chance that possibility.

The plan was that the earthworks before Richmond would be manned
by Magruder's troops who would be available for an offensive attack if
needed. Lee realized these daring plans would win only by their boldness
and not by the might of military arms for the infantry carried rifles and
muskets but many were armed with flintlocks and shotguns. Their older and
worn cannon could not match the rifled pieces of the Federals so they
definitely would have to rely on the cunning of the Commanders.

When Lee finished explaining his plans, he left the room. It was up
to the generals to do the planning of the maneuvers. Longstreet asked Jackson
when could he be ready and Jackson told him the 25th. Everything depended
on Jackson because no regiment or brigade could go forward until the General
got behind Porter and had turned his position. Longstreet thought Jackson
needed more time to do this. Finally, Jackson agreed to the 26th at three
o'clock.

The plan was settled and Jackson rode off to prepare for his move. The
Valley campaign had formerly come to an end and he was about to do bigger
and better things. The magnitude of the plan overwhelmed him but he was
ready for it. His Lord would lead him and he would succeed!

General Jackson and his Valley Army got to Ashland on July 25th. The
Federals had expected Jackson to appear at any time and he had not. Lincoln
was frantic as he had no idea where Jackson was.

By early morning of the 26th of June, 1862, the three Confederate
divisions of Ambrose Hill, Daniel Hill and Longstreet had advanced to the
Chickahominy bridges. They were ready to cross with Ambrose Hill in the
lead. Jackson was expected to attack Porter's position any minute. The
bridges would be released and they would not have to force a passage. But
nothing happened.

Hill's men stood on the Mechanicsville road just waiting to move.
Hours passed and still there was no sign of Jackson. A hot summer sun beat

down on the impatient infantry and they could hear the hiss and scream of shells as they were being hurled back and forth across the river. The dank and fetid ground stank of rot and the humidity drained their strength. Swamps lay everywhere and they could see the thick oaks and pines with tangled vines running up them to give a lush green roof over the river. It was a desolate wilderness.

Hill waited until three o'clock and when Jackson did not appear, he thought the whole plan had fallen through. Ambrose Hill lead an advance down the north bank of the river with Longstreet and D. H. Hill following. By late afternoon, Hill ordered an assault on the Federal position at Beaver Dam but they could not break through the swampy wooded creek. The enemy was on the other side!

Hill's men rushed frantically from their positions and ran right into the muzzles of the cannon. They were quickly shot down and fell into the creek or sank in the mired mud of the swamp. In just a half hour, over 2000 Confederates had met their death. The first part of the planned maneuver had met with a bloody and ignominious defeat.

I learned much later that Jackson's orders were to wait until Hill communicated with him and no word came. Porter saw Jackson as he began to advance but he knew there was no use in retreating until nightfall. He just sat back and rested with his men while they watched the disaster across the way.

By the following day, the Confederates had crossed the Chickahominy and were attacking Porter in his new defenses. Jackson had caught up with them and started the advance south from Hundley's Corner toward the old Walnut Grove Church and on to Cold Harbor which lay in the back of Porter's position. He calculated that Porter would have to retreat directly in front of him in order to reach safety at the White House. The trap was working and about to be sprung. Jackson rode forward to meet General Lee at Walnut Grove for another field meeting.

Lee met Jackson and they went over and sat down under the shade of some trees to discuss the plan. Lee told him to wait at Old Cold Harbor until the frontal attack on Porter drove him towards Jackson at which point Porter and his troops would be destroyed.

Jackson led his men on a round about way toward Old Cold Harbor to wait for the enemy to be driven his way. He saw that they had not budged and he could hear Hill's men fighting a desperate battle. He waited a bit and decided to throw in his and Daniel Hill's division to help the other Hill. They yelled as they crashed out of the woods and bending low charged up a steep hill and began to fire a volley of shots into the face of the enemy.

The Yankees scattered and retreated to the Chickahominy. The Battle of Gaines Mill was over.

At dawn on the 28th, Lee found a few Federal stragglers but never could pinpoint the position of Porter. By the 30th, they had crossed the Chickahominy and were trying to catch up with the Yankees. On and on they marched until they reached the top of Malvern Hill and found that General Porter and troops were in full retreat and out of reach of Confederate firepower. They also discovered that the Federal artillery was lined up battery by battery on top of a nearby hill.

Lee was sick when he found out about the Federals. Longstreet advised that they should attack and now the desperate Lee took his advice and ordered an attack at four thirty that afternoon. The infantry advanced, Daniel Hill's men charged across the swamps, Huger and Magruder launched another isolated assasult and after three hours, the Confederates had made no progress against them. Our situation was very bad and the opinion of the field command indicated hopelessness. It was a disaster and there was nothing but gloom in the Confederate army as they camped that night.

President Davis came down to talk with General Lee, Longstreet, Jackson, Major McGuire and Major Dabney. The discussion concerned McClellan, and as to whether or not he was retreating. No one seemed to know where he was. Jackson was not pleased with the way the meeting was going. They had experienced a severe setback. When the meeting was over, with nothing accomplished, Jackson took his staff and rode on to a farmhouse near the Willis Church, where they stayed the night.

Stonewall Jackson's rage had been building for two days. He heard that McClellan had gotten away so he took his staff and went back to their old base. The next day, July 8th, General Lee withdrew the Army of Northern Virginia to Richmond and the Seven Days' Battles were over.

McClellan's retreat meant the Army of Northern Virginia had stopped the Army of the Potomac, saved Richmond and brought an end to the second stage of General Lee's strategic plans for the expulsion of the enemy from Virginia. The price of victory had been costly. Lee had lost 20,000 men. The Yankees had been beaten back with brains...not arms. The Southern commander barely had 65,000 men to fight any battle. This had to be rectified soon. Lee called for reinforcements.

Jackson urged the immediate formation of an invading army which would go north into Maryland and Pennsylvania before John Pope, Lincoln's new Major General, could get there. He also recognized that Lincoln's concern was not Richmond, but Washington. He asked President Davis for permission to forge ahead but Davis was so shaky in his own capital, he only listened to Jackson's idea and promptly put it aside. It was apparent Lee and Jackson had to fight President Davis as well as the enemy.

Pope was an enemy to be reckoned with. He changed the Union forces completely, insulted the Southern people, their soldiers, treated all Southern raiders as guerillas, then shot them, and forced all civilians within the district to take an oath of allegiance to the "United States." If they refused, they were driven from their homes. He ordered the army to live off the land they had taken. They pillaged the supplies, then burned the homes and barns and generally tore up the countryside.

Jackson heard what he was doing and vowed to give Pope his full attention. He decided to lure him further south. By August 6th, Pope advanced from Sperryville towards Culpeper and the next day Jackson started after him. Although he didn't have enough cooperation from Hill, fortune smiled on him. He heard General Banks was traveling wtih Pope's army. Banks was eager for revenge against Jackson for what he had done to him at Winchester; he came rushing down through Virginia and attacked "Stonewall" at Cedar Mountain. They smashed the left flank of Jackson and put it to rout.

Jackson and Lee bided their time. Lincoln had sent McClellan's army around to reinforce Pope and by August 17th Lee's army of 55,000 was out of sight near the Rapidan River behind Clark's Mountain. Several scouts went out to get the two generals, escorting them to the crest of the mountain. There they could see, in the far distance the very bustling camps of the Federal army. Their glistening tents, guns and the wisps of smoke curling up from their campfires, told the two generals that the Yankees were just sitting there relaxing. They all but invited rapid destruction.

Lee ordered Stuart to ride over to Rappahannock Station and burn the bridge in the back of Pope. The orders were intercepted by the Yankees and Pope learned of Lee's plans. Longstreet groaned as he told Jackson what had happened but Stuart made up for the delay by capturing Pope's headquarters and brought back Pope's dispatch book. The information in it was of the greatest value and very revealing. It told of McClellan's army landing in Alexandria with 30,000 more men. This increased Pope's total to 100,000 men and when the rest of the army landed there, they would have 150,000.

Lee and Jackson held one of their now famous meetings on the afternoon of August 24th. Jackson was seen moving his left arm, palm turned out, then leaning down to draw maps with the toe of his boot. He seemed very excited as Lee was listening intently. Then they parted. No one knew what they were talking about as they both seemed happy.

Before first light of the next day, General Jackson and the entire corps of 23,000 men moved towards the ford on the upper Rappahannock at Hinson's Mill. They were walking in the pitch blackness, stumbling over roots and rocks and walking through the shallow waters just north of the flowing river. They had no idea where they were going. They were hungry but had been told they could expect a good hot meal and a change of clean drawers when the march was over.

Every twenty minutes, the march would stop and the men would rest for two minutes. Then up again and on until they had marched some twenty miles. They ate what they could find along the way. By midnight the column halted at Salem, rested and before dawn, breakfasted on green corn and were on their way again. By then every soldier knew he was marching in the back of Pope's army and the excitement grew. People brought food out to them. The grateful soldiers ate as they marched until they learned they were only 13 miles from the rear of Pope's army.

Jackson knew the odds were against him but he was not concerned. Near Gainesville, and much to the befuddled surprise of his troops, he did not go straight to Manassas, but went where the abundant and tremendous Federal warehouses lay and pillaged the whole thing. Now he had the base of Pope's supplies, food, clothing, transportation, arms, ammunition and Pope had nothing.

Jackson took his troops in to Manassas and found many areas of the village lined with open sheds, storehouses bursting with food, clothing and high mounds of cannon shells and round shot in long rows. His men were left to gorge on all of the good food and wash it down with Rhine wine. They found new clothes and shoes, even toothbrushes! It was a banquet such as might have been held in Rome. The happy men could bathe, dress, eat and then rest. The good meal they had been promised turned out to be a never-forgotten dinner complete with fresh and new clothing of all types to wear.

Pope finally got wind of Jackson's raid. Now he knew his foe was in the Valley. He did not realize the power of Jackson; thus he issued orders for his men to go to Gainesville and cut off the retreat. Pope went on to Bristoe and looked east to Manassas where he saw the red hot fires of the burning village and realized Jackson's whole corps of men had fallen in behind him. He lost his head and issued orders for intercepting Jackson. He had to defeat the terrible Stonewall!

Pope couldn't find Jackson yet he heard the sounds of muskets and the western sky was black with the smoke of battle. Then it dawned on him that Jackson was hidden in the woods west of the Warrenton Turnpike and had attacked King's division as it marched toward Centerville. Stonewall was up to his old tricks. Not only had he eluded his enemies but he had attacked one of their divisions! Now he realized the great Stonewall had come to destroy his whole army!

That night Pope issued an order for McDowell to intercept the retreat of the enemy. Sigel was in the front of Jackson and he could see no way the mighty Stonewall could escape. So far, Pope had done just what Jackson anticipated. Now he was going to bring his army west of Bull Run to the place where Stonewall had chosen to fight him.

Jackson had chosen the strongest position in the region. All of his fighting men were stationed around him on a line extending a mile and three quarters with five riflemen stationed to every yard. General Jackson stood on a hill overlooking the whole field and surveyed the battle area with his field glasses highly pleased at the shaping up of events.

The first attack struck A.P. Hill's sector and was beaten back badly. Other attacks followed and little by little, Pope's army was driven back. The battle raged, Pope had five assaults and had wrecked 30,000 of his infantry. By nightfall, the victory belonged to Jackson! The enemy had been driven back. Jackson's men fell back a few hundred yards to the woods on the top of the hill and they rested. Just around midnight, all fighting seemed to come to a halt as the wounded were screaming and the doctors worked to save them. They had beaten Pope but at what a price!

Dr. McGuire came late that night to Jackson's headquarters and said,

"General, this day has been won by nothing but bravery, physical courage and brilliant fighting."

"No, Doctor. It has been won by nothing but the blessing and protection of Providence."

On that hot morning of August 30th, General Pope sat back gloating. He was pleased that the attacks of yesterday had only deterred his men overnight. Now he had all 65,000 of them ready and waiting to destroy the General who had beaten him back the day before. He had heard that Jackson's right hand man, Longstreet, was nowhere near. This was good news indeed. It would be easier to take on Stonewall! Evidently, the enemy was whipped and he would punish them more today.

Meanwhile, the Confederates had rested and eaten. They were beginning to perk up and the reason was, they knew Longstreet and his 30,000 reinforcements were hiding in the woods just waiting for Pope to make a move. There was no doubt in any soldier's mind that their General had planned this move to confuse Pope.

Just before noon, General Pope went to the top of a hill near Stone House and looked down on the Warrenton Turnpike. There he saw his army just ready to attack the Rebels at the given signal. He had 20,000 infantry with 40,000 in the backwoods and ravines for support. He knew that he could crush Jackson who had only 17,000 men! And best of all, Longstreet was not there to be faced.

He gave the order to advance. At long last, Jackson was his!

Pope's army stepped along at a lively pace and after marching a few miles. they heard a Confederate bugle. Then other sounds came and they knew it was the sound of muskets. To their amazement they watched as heavy lines of gray infantry ran out from behind the hill and came down on them like a landslide.

Pope stood there and watched from afar as he saw his men go down under the enemy's bullets. He couldn't believe his eyes. Jackson had tricked him again. He had lured him on, out into the open where he could fire on his men. The mighty Stonewall had outdone him!

All afternoon the battle raged. Longstreet's men had hardly been called on to shoot but by four thirty, Jackson called for help. Longstreet was skillful. He knew just where to charge to do the most good and in the next few hours turned several batteries on the Federals with a flanking fire. He drove them down into the valley where they huddled, then broke and fled pell mell in every direction.

Longstreet's men poured out of their hiding places near the Warrenton Turnpike and with their own Rebel yell charged mightily into the lines around the right wing of the Federals. Jackson's men, weary, without rest from three days of fighting, rushed across the deep ravine while 45,000 of Lee's men moved in like a tidal wave. Forward like a flood, with bayonets glittering in the late afternoon sun.

Artillerymen drove their horses until they frothed at the mouth, plunging through the infantry in a frenzied heat. The massed guns were booming over their heads. While this battle was raging, Stuart brought his horsemen in and led the charge. Never was the fighting so fierce as it was that late afternoon.

By ten o'clock that night, Pope's army had been driven back across Bull Run and the battle of Second Manassas was over. Jackson had won a convincing and smashing victory!

Pope was completely demoralized. He retreated to Washington and his Army of Virginia ceased to exist merging with the Army of the Potomac.

General Robert E. Lee's original plan for fighting and winning had been successful. He had driven the enemy away from the Southern Capitol. His losses had been great for 9000 Confederates had fallen at Manassas, a severe blow to the manpower of the Southern armies, but the enemy had suffered much more. In the combined two campaigns that Lee had mounted, the Northern armies lost 33,000 men, 82 guns, 58,000 rifles, many batteries of cannon, tremendous stores of ammunition, shells, drugs, food, clothing and large quantitites of war material badly needed by the Confederate forces.

President Davis viewed the results of the two great battles with an air of complacency and nonchalance, but not General Lee. He had promised Jackson he would move to invade Maryland and he intended to keep his word. The Supreme Commander of all the Southern armies and his right hand, Lieutenant General Jackson were about to engage in an endeavor which would require all of their military expertise and experienced know how of all battles in which they had been engaged to this point.

Chapter 12

Panic and pandemonium reigned in Washington! President Lincoln and the War Cabinet had counted heavily on Pope's Army of Virginia overcoming whatever opposition the Confederates could muster against them, yet it was Pope and the Union forces who were smashed and forced to retreat back beyond the Potomac. Sleepless nights for Lincoln were increased as the long suffering and gaunt President paced his study floor pondering the loss of so many young men in a war that apparently had no foreseeable end. When and where would the Federal forces claim victory over the South? Obviously there was something wrong in the manner in which Federal commanders were appointed because Union leadership up to this point was a dismal failure! The strategy designed by his generals and War Cabinet was lacking in execution that should have by this time brought some victories. As the situation presented itself, the Confederates were all victorious in Virginia, the entry door to Washington, creating a perilous situation for the Federal government in the North and East portions of the United States. With magnificent leadership and outstanding generalship, Robert E. Lee and ''Stonewall'' Jackson of the Confederacy defeated every general and military strategy that the North had thrown against them. Something had to be done to recoup from the damaging blows that the South had inflicted on the power of all the military might of the North!

Lincoln decided to call a War Cabinet meeting jointly with his military staff and advisors. He spoke softly but firmly as he outlined the problems of finding a winning field commander, urging each of his Cabinet members to think carefully of some member of the military who could in their opinion successfully lead the Union armies to victory in Virginia. He pointed out that a crucial point had been reached in the war and something must be done to stop Lee and Jackson before the North defeated itself by continuing losses to the South.

Among those present at this meeting, was Hiram Brainer, a minor official of the War Department, and a man who had made many enemies among those contractors trying to do business with the Government who either tried to foist second rate goods or poorly manufactured products on the military establishment which were so badly needed by the army and navy to conduct the War against the Confederates. Furthermore, he was arbitrary and uncompromising, using his position as a lever to get his way wherever and whenever possible. He helped enforce the unpopular draft laws without compassion or pity on extreme hardship cases. He so restricted the media, that at times they printed information as helpful to the enemy as any that his best spies could obtain from the South. He had spies all over the North and South and was not beyond the limits of keeping a straight face and speaking loftily about honesty, morals and the very law itself, even though he and his hirelings were bending or breaking every law of the land. He was also devious to the extent that all of his under the counter operations were covered up, even though said operations might have been in the best interests of the government.

Brainer frequently quarreled with his superiors, ridiculing them behind their backs for what he considered weakness or compromises on carrying on the War. Despite their many differences from time to time, they all worked as a team, serving the common cause and using one another's strength to compliment the deficiencies of each other. They all understood him even though they did not always agree on how the War should be conducted. Even the President of the United States had his differences with Secretary of War Stanton, but still worked with him in the common cause. In short, Hiram Brainer was a patriot of great administrative abilities but a forceful, persuasive and dangerous man.

Considering that Brainer was a very blunt person, extremely intelligent, convinced of his own acquired power and accustomed to dealing with people who could be persuaded for the right amount to carry out any mission he assigned them, is it any wonder that Lincoln's challenge to him and the other War Cabinet members came at just the right moment? The moment was right because the President felt that defeat after defeat by the South rocked the very foundation of his government in Washington. How would the nation react to a continuance of this tremendous loss in manpower, monetary cost and prestige, while the European countries on the sidelines watched as the Union was jolted in battle after battle?

As Lincoln talked, Brainer listened attentively and the wheels began to spin in his mind. The South kept winning because of Lee and Jackson plus the super dedicated fighting ability of the soldiers they led. Take the leaders away and estimate what would happen then. Yes sir, it was an original possibility! The more he thought about it, the better the idea appealed to him. But, ah, how does one implement an undertaking of that type? Lincoln should be notified, but no, such a proposal would appear to him as unethical, against the rules of warfare, criminal, and too risky a chance to be taken. What then should be done? The answer as he saw it was kidnapping, imprisonment or assassination.

There would be no information given to the President on this venture. Just as Brainer and his confidants had done on other occasions where extreme secrecy and underhanded tactics were employed, the matter would be covered up so that no one including the President would know what occurred. The method would have to be worked out in finest detail, the right people bought, and when the affair was concluded, all members who perpetrated the action would be smuggled out of the country with plenty of gold to purchase their silence.

Now came the problem of the method to be used and what people would have to be contacted. Brainer kept a secret and confidential diary of every spy, rogue, hooligan or assassin ever employed by him plus other names or persons who wanted a chance to show what they could do. Each name was carefully scrutinized and put on a separate list if he or she had possibility to carry out the project. Brainer had eliminated all the usual means of kidnapping, ransom and/or disappearance. He was convinced that the only way to eliminate Lee and Jackson was by kidnapping, secret imprisonment, or assassination. Without General Robert E. Lee as Commander In Chief and General Thomas Jonathan "Stonewall" Jackson, his top field commander, the armies of the Confederacy, tried and tested as they were would be impotent and subject to destruction by the North. Brainer estimated that their worth to the Southern armies was the equivalent of an entire army corps. A stroke of this kind would be a great morale booster for the generals and soldiers of the new armies that the North would send against the South, assuring themselves of victory and the ultimate surrender of the Confederacy. And just imagine what it would do for the people of the North, who could begin to look forward to peace and reconstruction!

Secret messages went out to those persons selected by Brainer for this project; so secretive that even the ultimate message delivered was not understood by any of the hirelings employed. Brainer had access to several hundred thousands in gold thus assuring his finances for the plot. The group came into Washington one by one, using false papers and different names, all provided by Brainer. Among these persons, were two deserters from one of the Virginia regiments who were part of Jackson's First Brigade. These deserters were wanted by Jackson and his command and orders had been issued to shoot them upon sight if they were located. It was very obvious that wanted men of this type would risk most anything to escape execution by the Confederates. Brainer knew this, and after culling his lists, he selected these two for the job of kidnapping Lee and General Jackson. Their names were Slim Jaggert and Hank Babick. Both men had been arrested and served terms in the army stockade for cowardice under fire, desertion of posts, drunkenness and insulting officers.

Another pair, George Crandon and Black Eye Carlson were to be members of the team with Jaggert and Babick. Each appeared in an out of the way hotel in Washington before Mr. Hiram Brainer, and questioned closely about their willingness to carry out the plan as outlined by Brainer's men, with the understanding that each one would be shipped out of the country when the job was done and would find themselves richer by $50,000 in gold. They were also given to understand that they would be watched very closely by other members of the plot so that any false move by any of them would mean immediate death. Each man was sworn to secrecy.

Brainer's orders were rehearsed, studied and consigned to each one's memory. The deadline for the plan was August 31st, 1862. If the plot succeeded, both Lee and Jackson would be taken to a designated spot, turned over to other members of the group who would in turn get their orders directly from Brainer.

It did not take too long for the plotters to complete their plans. Jaggert and Babick had a hideaway in the rural area outside of Washington, to where they and their friends retired for loafing and drinking. One of the revelers noted that Jaggert kept teasing Babick about what he would do with his gold after he received it. Both were drunk, and while partying, said some things that a certain reveler thought was odd and not in conformity with how these two deserters lived. Joe Hall, the reveler in question was a Northerner who had sympathy for the South. Neda, was an acquaintance who now and then furnished him with a good bottle of whiskey for news that might be important. Without hesitancy, Hall revealed to her the odd remarks that Jaggert and Babick were spouting the night he went to their party.

Neda had heard many things in her interest in obtaining important information for her Southern friends and this news intrigued her. She could not quite understand why Jaggert and Babick were getting the sum of gold that her friend, Joe Hall, told her about. Since they were deserters from Jackson's old Brigade, she assumed it had something to do with Jackson's 2nd Corps and perhaps Jackson himself. Nothing had been said about General Robert E. Lee, but she again assumed that $50,000 in gold, a king's ransom, would not be paid just for one person or even a military genius like General "Stonewall" Jackson. This was a matter too serious to take any chances with; she must immediately contact General Jeb Stuart and General Jackson's aide, Captain Caleb Joshua Sparks! A discussion and decision of action would have to take place as soon as possible. Neda knew that she would have to learn more about Jaggert and Babick's windfall before she could meet with Stuart and me, and set about to make their acquaintance.

Beautiful as she was, Neda determined to dress as a common strumpet and hang around certain drinking parlors where Jaggert and Babick spent a great deal of their time. She knew that with the type of clothes she wore, the heavy makeup, perfume and the undulations of her very feminine form, she would attract attention. At the "Cry of the Wolf" saloon, even the drunks who were in a stupor paid attention to this beautiful and luscious morsel of womanhood who tripped into the premises giggling and singing bawdy songs. Everyone wanted to know who she was and where she came from. When Jaggert and Babick came in, their buddies pointed her out to them, praising her looks, curves and laughing mouth. It didn't take long for Neda and the tools of Hiram Brainer to get acquainted. Neda forced herself to keep up with the drinking of Jaggert and Babick, slyly pouring as much on to the floor as she could without being noticed. By this time, the two men were quite inebriated and almost asleep.

Neda had arranged in advance for a carriage to meet her nearby the saloon, and it was waiting, when arm in arm with Jaggert and Babick she left the drinking parlor. In the carriage she proposed that they go to their hideaway for more drinks and celebration. When the men saw the several bottles of good bond whiskey which she had thoughtfully stored in the carriage, whatever suspicions they had of her were gone. Jaggert and Babick looked forward to a great time of drinking and rollicking with this gorgeous and sweet smelling woman.

After bouncing along in the carriage over the rough roads, they arrived at the hideaway in the early hours of the morning. Neda quietly told the driver to pull around out of sight and wait for her no matter how long it took. The carriage driver, having been paid well in advance, did as he was told. Neda and the men went inside, where the first order of business was to break open the bonded whiskey that she had provided for the occasion.

Again, Neda feigned drinking the fiery liquid, while Jaggert and Babick downed glass after glass. Soon, Babick dropped off in a deep sleep while Jaggert, his arms around Neda, drank and kissed her as though she was his very own. The more he kissed her, the more aroused he became and Neda encouraged him on, returned his amorous advances in a teasing manner. She opened her bodice and Jaggert lost all control of himself. Now was the time that Neda had planned to get Jaggert to tell her what the gold windfall was all about. Overcome with lust at the sight of her breasts, the taste of her lips and the close embraces, driven to the edge by the consumed whiskey, Jaggert talked about the plan to kidnap Generals Lee and Jackson and how it would be accomplished. Neda stroked his head and face while she got him to talk as much as she could. Lulled into quietude by Neda's stroking, Jaggert gradually fell into a deep sleep. She quietly lowered him to a sleeping position on the bed, gathered her things, dressed and left the hideaway. Urging the carriage driver to drive as fast as he could, she directed him to a rendezvous where she got off an important message to General Jeb Stuart and me to meet her as quickly as possible on a matter of the greatest importance.

At the hideaway, Jaggert and Babick slept like logs. The intake of whiskey had been so great that all they could recall the next morning was that they had a wonderful time and that Neda had really been responsible for a night to remember. All events of the prior evening were forgotten; neither of the men were aware that they had talked anything at all about the secret mission to which they had been sworn. Even the spies of Brainer who watched Jaggert and Babick were not aware of what Neda had learned.

The carriage raced through the night on darkened roads emptied of traffic much earlier in the evening. Neda could barely contain herself as she watched the miles reel off in the stygian darkness. Her driver was very familiar with the highway and recognized the various landmarks that marked the way to the appointed house in which Neda was to meet Stuart and me. At long last, just before dawn broke and the first rays of light were coming up, she spied the house from the carriage and had her driver drop her off at the entrance. As she stepped down from the carriage she noted the beautiful brown stallion, with cavalry insignia and the sleek black mare that were the respective horses of General Stuart and myself.

Stepping into the house, she was greeted by both of us, politely embracing and expressing joy of seeing each other so soon after her message had reached our camps. Tired and exhausted as she was after such a hectic night, she couldn't contain herself and began talking as fast as she could pointing out the danger that Generals Lee and Jackson were facing. Stuart courteously offered her a glass of brandy to help overcome her fatigue and I fluffed the pillows on the sofa so that she could relax while she relayed the news. Both of us asked many questions trying to find out all we could about the plan of Brainer to do away with the South's two greatest heroes, and the villains appointed to carry out the dastardly acts.

Having revealed all that she could and warning Stuart and me that this was not just a plan on paper but an action that Brainer's men intended to carry out, before September 1st, she added that in all likelihood, the rogues would disguise themselves by cutting off beards and mustaches, wearing wigs and dressing up in current Confederate uniforms. To protect Lee and Jackson, the Confederates would have to devise a plan to counter everything Brainer's men planned to do. Of greatest important was the security to be established around both Generals. Additional sentries and officers of the guard would have to be posted in and around the tents or quarters of Lee and Jackson with special emphasis placed on sharpshooters—the best in the Army of Northern Virginia. Lee and Jackson were to be informed and requested to play their roles as suggested by Stuart and me.

Neda was profusely thanked by both of us and we left to begin the work of implementing the counter plan. She was reminded that her bravery and help for the Southern cause would not be forgotten and that Generals Lee and Jackson would be made aware of what she had done for them and the Army of Northern Virginia.

Meanwhile, Jaggert and Babick together with the duo of George Crandon and Black Eye Carlson were not idle. They met at their hideaway, discussing how the jobs would be done. Jaggert and Babick proposed to dress in new Confederate uniforms, new boots, caps, side arms with the insignia of the medical group emblazoned on their uniform coats and caps. They intended to get into Jackson's camp posing as doctors with forged papers indicating a transfer to the Second Corps. The fastest horses that Brainer could obtain would be placed at their disposal and kept close by for the escape with Jackson in their custody. The action would be rehearsed and rehearsed until every detail was timed down to the last second. They were to shoot anyone who challenged them and were to make their way with Jackson to the appointed river destination where strong rowers woud transport them and their prisoner across the Potomac and into the Union lines. Safely in the Union lines, with Jackson blindfolded and tied hand and foot, they were to deliver him into the hands of other agents of Brainer who then would take the prisoner to a predetermined and secret destination. Their part in the plot ended at that point as they were to make their way as rapidly as possible to a port on the East coast for transportation to another part of the world. If in the execution of their kidnap plan, they were surprised or apprehended, they were to shoot or stab General Jackson to death and do the best they could to escape, as under those circumstances they would be strictly on their own.

Crandon and Black Eye Carlson were to kidnap General Lee, using the same tactics as Jaggert and Babick used against General Jackson. Both operations were timed to occur on the same night at the same hour. Expediency was an absolute necessity and everything had to run like clockwork; any faltering would result in failure of the mission on either end of the plot. Brainer drummed into these villains the necessity of capturing both Generals; however, if only one was captured and brought out alive, it would be better than a complete failure. Crandon and Carlson were also enjoined to shoot or stab General Lee to death if they were surprised or apprehended in the act of trying to kidnap him. Both groups were assured by Brainer that the $50,000 in gold for each would be waiting at their destinations overseas after they left the country.

Stuart and I met with Generals Lee and Jackson and outlined the plot to them. We were granted the authority to set up special security forces in each respective camp, with sentries, officers of the guard and highly qualified sharpshooters stationed in strategic spots out of sight. The Generals were brave men and had dodged death many times on the battlefield displaying heroic form in front of their troops. What they faced now was obviously an outright kidnapping and possible death at the hands of the Brainer villains! Ordinary men might have been overtaken by fear; not Generals Lee and Jackson. Both were firm believers in God and trusted His Divine protection in every situation.

Lee and Jackson were urged to act in their usual normal manner as though nothing was amiss. When the villains entered the camp, they were to be directed to each General's quarters in the usual military manner according to the code of the army of Northern Virginia. In Jackson's camp, I would accompany Jaggert and Babick to the General's tent, backed up by normal acting sentries and guards. No chances were to be taken—the moment the villains entered Jackson's quarters, it was to be surrounded with top troops ready to apprehend or kill the two deserters. If I noticed any movement by Jaggert and Babick toward Jackson, I was to shoot both without any hesitancy. This very same procedure was set up for General Lee's camp, with General Jeb Stuart accompanying Crandon and Carlson into Lee's presence.

The evening of August 31, 1862 was warm and pleasant. Moonlight shone on all of the roads leading into the camps of both Generals. The troops were relaxing, having had their supper, smoking, playing cards or checkers, and peacefully enjoying the lovely night. Other than the arrangements made in advance by General Stuart and me, all appeared to be normal. Jackson had just concluded a prayer service with his aides and sat down at his field table to write up the log for the day. Over in Lee's camp, the General was studying maps of the terrain of Maryland, estimating that a full campaign could be conducted in that salient before the fall weather set in.

The clop clop of horses' hooves could be heard alongside the road leading into both camps. The moment that the plotters and the defenders had awaited was rapidly approaching. Jaggert and Babick tried to assume an air of calm and relaxed demeanor as they rode along the entrance to Jackson's camp. Challenged by the sentries they gave the correct password and entered the enclosure. Their papers were examined and an escort guided them toward the tent of the General. The guards around General Jackson's tent had received the previously agreed upon signals that the villains were in camp and on their way to the General. One could almost feel the electric tension of the moment!

As Jaggert and Babick followed the officer guiding them to Jackson's tent, their hands were itching for a fast draw of revolvers for the planned surprise attack on the General as well as disposal of the officer leading them. Just as the tent flap was opened, Jaggert went for his gun while Babick whirled around and grappled with the guide officer in front of him. A figure emerged from the shadow behind the table where Jackson was supposedly sitting and within a split second a tremendous flash was seen and two loud shots were heard. Jaggert dropped like a poled steer, his revolver still clutched in his right hand. He was dead before his body hit the floor of the tent. I had killed Jaggert before he could even press the trigger of his gun! The second shot from my gun caught Babick in the center of his forehead, killing him instantly, his body falling against the Confederate officer who had lunged for the ground just before I fired. The person sitting at the table was not General Jackson, but a dummy, dressed in the General's uniform and made up to resemble the commanding officer of the 2nd Corps. The shots brought soldiers running from all sides, but the officers of the guard held everyone back in accordance with the prearranged plan of Stuart and myself. No one outside the circle of those who had been informed in advance were to know about this attempt on Jackson's life. The bodies were secretly taken out and disposed of in lime pits outside of the army's perimeter.

Over at General Lee's headquarters, the same closely watched proceedings were taking place. As Crandon and Carlson rode up to the General's camp, they too were challenged by sentries and produced forged papers for inspection. Once they had been cleared for entry into the compound, the signal was slyly passed on to the officers of the guard and General Jeb

Stuart. Everyone acted calmly, just as the prearranged plan called for, and George Crandon and Black Eye Carlson were escorted in by an officer who acted as their guide. When General Lee's tent flap was opened, the villains saw a figure sitting at a desk, slightly bent over and apparently writing reports. The lamplight in the tent reflected his shadow against the canvas wall and it was obvious to Crandon and Carlson that General Lee had not heard them come in. But others hidden in the tent had heard and seen the approach of both men. Crandon pulled his gun, pointing it at Lee's head and started to say something, when a terrible boom was heard and clutching his chest, Crandon fell to the ground, mortally wounded. Stuart's horse pistol and his pin point accuracy had removed Crandon as a threat to the General. Black Eye Carlson had pulled a knife just as his co-conspirator was pulling his gun, with the intent of removing the officer guide in front of him by stabbing him in the back. His knife never touched the officer guide as a shot rang out from the side of the tent from the rifle of one of the sharpshooters, catching Black Eye in the right temple, killing him on the spot. Both Crandon and Carlson were dead and their threat removed for good.

The shots brought men running, but the officers of the guard kept all the curious back and removed the bodies secretly in canvas bags. A few soldiers had been sworn to secrecy and were used only for the purpose of removing the two dead men and disposing of their remains. Crandon and Carlson were buried in a pit fifteen feet deep, all their personal belongings and identification removed so that no one would ever be able to identify the remains if by chance their bodies were dug up at a future date, with no stone or marker over their grave.

Reports were handed down by the Confederate command, that several deserters were caught in the environs of the camp and were shot on sight. No word was ever published or distributed in the Southern papers as the Generals felt it would be in the best interests of the Confederate cause that the perpetrators of the dastardly plot up North knew nothing of what occurred. Mr. Brainer, the man of the North, who had hoped to be branded a hero by Lincoln and the cabinet, suffered the agonies of his loss and shortly thereafter, without revealing any of his malevolent machinations, resigned from his position in the War Department.

Generals Lee and Jackson, were made aware of Neda's help in revealing the plot, and gratefully sent her letters in which they expressed their thanks. General Jeb Stuart and I received letters of commendation and personal handshake thanks for our respective parts in handling the entire affair.

At this point, General Lee turned his attention to the contemplated campaign for an invasion of Maryland and establishment of a future base for a drive into the North. There were many advantages to a successful invasion of this neighboring state, particularly in winning over more soldiers for the Confederate armies as well as an additional supply ground for needed food, guns, ammunition, etc. He would have to meet with Jackson and outline his commitment for such an invasion. Jackson would know just how Lee wanted it carried out!

Chapter 13

General Lee held to his promise. On the morning of September 2, 1862, Jackson received orders from General Lee to start the Maryland invasion. He would be supported by Generals Hill, Lafayette McLaws, another division under General John Walker and Wade Hampton's cavalry. Jackson looked at the letter and noted that the number of men totaled 65,000 men. He knew better for many of the men had left and gone home.

After the two battles at Manassas, many of the men were very war weary. They had not been home for months, nor had they seen their families. Many of them needed to attend to their farms. Jackson could not count on them coming back. He knew he would have at the most 50,000 men who were seasoned and trained for battle.

President Davis had been of no help to Lee. He didn't think Lee needed to invade the East. He wanted to concentrate on the West although Lee had written and told him the army was not properly equippd to invade enemy territory without increased armaments, munitions, food and trained troops. Lee was determined to press on because the invasion of Maryland would be worth the effort. He hoped to free the oppressed little state and add recruits to his army. Also, an invasion would draw the Federals away from Richmond and free the people of Virginia to harvest their crops and send supplies to him. He knew one victory in the North's territory would be equal to five in Virginia.

On the 6th of September, Jackson's men, followed by Hill's fresh recruits, marched into the little town of Leesburg. Many of them were barefoot, their clothes torn and ragged and their beards covered with lice.

The people who lined the sidewalks to watch them walk into town wondered if they really were soldiers.

Lee concentrated his troops in a wooded lot called Best's Grove. He established his headquarters there with Jackson and Longstreet in tents close by. Lee imposed a rigid discipline about the town of Frederick which was eight miles down the road. Guards were posted at the town limits and soldiers were forbidden to enter without passes.

Jackson found admirers in Maryland. The people brought him gifts, with one being a powerful gray mare which was a substitute for Little Sorrel who had been stolen. Jackson mounted the mare and she reared and fell. Jackson was thrown to the ground and knocked unconscious. When he revived, he had a searing pain in his back and was unable to move. Doctors feared he had an injury to his spine. They took him to their field hospital and kept him until he was able to walk again. Although he did not suffer permanent injury he was in great pain; he could not perform his duties and turned the command over to D. H. Hill while he recuperated.

Lee, in the meantime, was trying to make a decision about the invasion. He had moved his line of supply from Eastern Virginia to Staunton by way of Harper's Ferry. Now he must either capture or fight the garrison of Yankees at Harper's Ferry. The Federal army was following him but they were so far away, he would have time to send a detachment to clear up the rear. The orders of the Confederate manuevers went out to Jackson, Longstreet and Hill as "Special Orders No. 191." It would divide his army into three sections.

September 10th Jackson moved out. He had his own three divisions; McLaws, Richard Anderson and John Walker with a combined force of some 23,000. As the troops moved out of Frederick, Jackson and his staff took the lead. By the 12th they had reached Williamsport. They were reversing their tracks and entering Virginia soil once more on a march even worse than any they had taken. He soon learned that the Yankee garrison had, indeed, fled to Harper's Ferry and all he had to do was march to Harper's Ferry, surround it and force a surrender.

Jackson moved into Martinsburg and established headquarters in the hotel. He was almost mobbed by a group of well wishers. The ladies came up to kiss and hug him, telling him how wonderful he was. One little girl wanted a button off of his coat as a memento and another wanted a piece of braid. He obligingly gave it to her but put his foot down when the ladies wanted a lock of his hair. He knew it was time to retreat and lock himself behind closed doors.

Slowly the Confederate troops completely encircled Harper's Ferry and by the 13th of September they had the entire Federal garrison surrounded and entrapped.

On the same day, McClellan, who had command of the old Pope forces, had moved into Frederick, and learned that Jackson had moved to Harper's Ferry. Longstreet was at Hagerstown and the troops of Daniel Hill held the pass at Turner's Gap on South Mountain through which McClellan's army would have to fight to reach the battle area. What was McClellan's next move? They were soon to find out.

The next morning 70,000 Federals advanced on Turner's Gap; 20,000 more under General Franklin struck at the pass below. This meant McClellan would now be between the two Confederate corps. The fighting began on the 14th when the Federals' advance guard struck out at Hill's division. Hill held the pass all day but was greatly outnumbered and all he could hope for was to hold position, until Lee and Jackson could unite. Longstreet's men came along to reinforce him, then retreated westward across Antietam Creek and took up a position at Sharpsburg.

Jackson was carefully getting his troops into position at Harper's Ferry on the morning of the 14th. He could hear the roar of battle at South Mountain and he knew McClellan was approaching. There was no time to lose to get to Lee so they could bring the three sections together. Walker went ahead and made the Federals attack him by exposing two of his regiments. The fighting lasted all day and the Yankees were caught up in a trap. The next morning the Federals surrendered 12,5000 men, 13,000 rifles and 73 cannon; Jackson was there to receive the surrender. Some of the prisoners saluted him and he returned their gesture.

The question coming to Jackson's mind was how did McClellan move so fast? Lee had expected him to move cautiously. What neither of them knew was that a soldier had carelessly taken Lee's "Special Order No. 191 thinking they were scraps of paper, and had wrapped three cigars in them, then tossed the paper away. Some Federal officer picked it up and dispatched it to McClellan thus giving him all the information he needed about the movement of the Confederate troops. The Confederate army could have been ruined because of this act.

General Lee looked through his fieldglass and saw McClellan's 90,000 men filing through the passes of South Mountain. Back down the road he had 16,000 of his men and the rest of the army was far away. In fact, too far away to help fight McClellan. He knew a battle must be fought before his army returned to Virginia yet he would wait as long as he could to send his men against this great Yankee force. He sat there waiting and pondering the plight of his situation.

The Confederate line ran from the Potomac on the left to a westward loop of the Antietam on the right. There was a great disadvantage to this position, for if he was defeated, he would have to retreat over the Potomac and while his men were wading through the water, they could be annihilated. There was still one small chance he could launch a counter-stroke and shatter McClellan's army and maybe the risk was not as great as it appeared. After all, his men were strong, seasoned veterans. They could end the war here and for such an end, he might take the risk.

Jackson and Walker crossed the Potomac at Shepherdstown and rode into Sharpsburg on the 16th. Then, other divisions reported, McLaws, Richard Anderson's and Ambrose Hill came in behind them. The lookouts had reported that McClellan's Army was crossing Antietam Creek and an attack might start that afternoon. Now Lee had 25,000 men ready and he decided to stay and fight!

There was a quiet air of expectancy as everyone waited for the battle to begin. Lee, Jackson and Longstreet stayed in the house all afternoon studying a map of Maryland. Other than a shell or two whizzing over them, the soldiers watched and waited for McClellan.

McClellan and his army crossed the creek and by morning the guns were thundering. Lee's men were waiting for them and when the Yankees came in view, they jumped up and ran forward. With only a force of 25,000 men, they fought McClellan and held their own. Lee had fooled McClellan who thought the great Southern General had at least 50,000 men and he dared not advance another inch. By late afternoon, Jackson's two divisions came in as reinforcements and Hood's division went to the rear to cook and eat. As a result, Jackson's men filled in for Hood's.

There were Confederate soldiers everywhere! Jackson north of Sharpsburg, the Stonewall Brigade to the left, Lawton's division in a corn field near the east woods, while Daniel Hill's lay in a sunken road. To the south in front of the town, lay Longstreet's men, Evans' brigade and the division of D. R. Jones with General Walker's division in reserve. Lee knew the battle would begin at dawn and he wondered if McLaws, Anderson and Ambrose Hill would get there in time to help them.

The lines were set throughout the night as shells flew back and forth. The men slept and often woke with a start only to fall back into a fitful sleep. Some wondered if they would live through the next day while the others prayed for protection.

The fire increased as the first few rays from a rising sun cast a beam of light across the corn fields. By 5:30, Hooker's 12,500 men came out of the North Woods and made their way northeast of the Hagerstown Pike. They advanced steadily and the Confederates launched fire. The Yankees were fighting desperately and were pushing the Confederates back. This continued for three hours and came to a halt. Jackson had used only 5,000 men and through a bold counter-stroke had driven them back through the North Woods.

But the battle was not over. In a few minutes Jackson saw Mansfield's men coming forward and sent word to Early's brigade to advance to the far left to his support. The Confederates were being steadily beaten back and by nine o'clock, Jackson had a wide gap in his line.

On and on the Yankees came as the battle grew fiercer. Lee ordered Walker's division to leave Longstreet and go to the support of Jackson. As they marched toward Jackson, they saw McLaw's and Anderson's divisions coming in. This gave Jackson a reserve of nearly 10,000 men.

Lee watched the procession as Jackson positioned himself at the Dunkard Church and sat there waiting, sucking a lemon and apparently lost in deep thought. He could see that the Yankees had broken his line but they had fallen down, exhausted and seemed content to do nothing. By ten o'clock, Hooker and Mansfield's men were out of the fight and Sedgwick was going through the cornfield into the West Woods.

It was there in the West Woods that Walker and McLaws caught up with Sedgwick and cut his men down like wheat. 2200 of them lay dead. Jackson was now riding with McLaws, when he heard the Confederate yell of victory.

"God has been very good to us today!"

Some 14,000 men were badly shaken but victorious. They reestablished lines north of the Dunkard Church and waited for a new attack which did not come. The reason was Hooker's and Mansfield's corps and Sedgwick's division lay dead or dying. Their units had ceased to exist. They had lost about 35,000 infantry.

Hill's men were still crouching on the sunken road. The Federals began another hard battle which came to an abrupt end by the Yankees' short success and a collapse a short time later. By twelve thirty, General Jackson was planning again. He calmly ate apples from a nearby tree and asked Walker to spare him about 5,000 men, then gave the order to his troops,

"When you hear Stuart's guns, advance. Our whole left wing will advance at the same time. We will drive McClellan into the Potomac!"

The plans went awry as the day passed. The Federals were secure on the Potomac and the three generals were grieving because they could not take 39,000 men and annihilate 90,000 Federals. They had to concede that the Yankees were too much for them that day. The Confederates dropped in fatigue and lay there exhausted.

The scene was one of gloom.

The story was the same from each officer who came up to Lee. Each division had been virtually wiped out and they could fight no more.

Lee turned to them and said,

"Gentlemen, we will not cross the Potomac tonight. Go collect your men and take them to the rear then strengthen your lines. If McClellan wants to fight in the morning, I will give him a battle."

Lee began to recoup his losses of the day before as 6000 men caught up with him. He felt better as he looked out over the rolling hills around Sharpsburg and saw thousands of glistening bayonets and long rows of cannon. Not a shot was being fired from either side yet there was an air of excitement again.

Maybe his fears of the night before had been groundless. Maybe his decision to invade Maryland would end the war. At least he was not willing to retreat without trying to shatter McClellan. He hoped that something would come up to change the tide of events. It did a few minutes later, when a courier came up to Colonel Stephen Lee with a note from Jackson, asking Lee to meet him right away. He mounted his horse and followed the courier to where Jackson was waiting.

"Colonel Lee, I want you to take a ride with me."

They traveled down a road away from the Dunkard Church finally cresting an open ridge with low lying brush near the extreme left of the Confederate line.

"Take your glasses, Colonel, and examine the Federal line."

Lee looked at the line which was supported by artillery.

"There is a large force there, General."

"Yes, and I want you to take fifty guns and crush that force."

Colonel Lee looked at the enemy again and told Jackson he could not crush such forces with fifty guns and the troops we had available.

Jackson's analysis coincided with Colonel Lee's, an expert on such situations. He was satisfied that the Confederate army was so reduced it lacked the power to fight another decisive battle in the area. They rode back to camp jointly convinced there would be no more fighting in the area.

The forces of General Lee crossed over into Virginia by nightfall of September 19th. At the same time, McClellan had sent General Porter and his corps across the river toward Washington. The Confederate Army fell back to Winchester to regroup and consolidate its strength for the coming battles ahead! Antietam and Sharpsburg were victories but terribly costly to the Southern cause!

All day we waited for another attack. None came. That night a raging storm came up and the whole Federal army retreated across the river. They were sent back to gain strength and a new commander. On the 16th of December, Burnside admitting defeat, asked for a truce which was granted. The battle was over.

General Jackson moved his headquarters to Moss Neck, eleven miles out of Fredericksburg and his men went back to their former stations. The hunting lodge he used was a one room house. It was furnished with a bed, table and several chairs. There was a stove for cooking and a long table for eating. He could double its use by working on it by day. Jim was perfectly happy with the arrangement and was quite pleased to bed down in a little ante room. I had my quarters in a log cabin just outside the General's door.

Our winter quarters were soon set up. The men built log cabins on the surrounding ground and although the condition of the army was bad and food was scarce, they managed to keep up their morale. The men built a simple log church where the chaplains could hold services. There was regular time set up for prayer meetings, special meetings, and on occasion, the death of some unfortunate soldier who never got over his wounds. The men never missed a service and seemed to gain inspiration from hearing the words of the Lord.

Christmas Day, General Stonewall Jackson became the host of a dinner party for the highest ranking officers. Jim prepared a fine turkey dinner with oysters and sweet potatoes. He made some of his cornbread and rolls, then topped the dinner off with some delicious cheese pie. Many of the local people had sent presents of food, with one lady sending a large tin of fresh butter. This was a treat for they had not seen butter for a long time. The men enjoyed a carefree day in the warm lodge. Each man felt the pangs of homesickness for family and friends but there was no way to get home until spring.

All through the winter Jackson stayed busy with various projects. Captain Hotchkiss came in and drew a large map of the area from Rapidan to Harrisburg. Jackson seemed to anticipate the need for such a map and as usual, he was right.

When spring came, Anna wrote to her husband and told him she was planning a visit. She wanted to bring little Julia to see her father. By April, Anna, accompanied by her maid, came up from North Carolina for a short visit. Jackson was in good spirits all the week before and by the time Anna arrived, he could hardly contain himself. He met her and proudly went about showing off his new daughter. They went up to Hamilton's Crossing near Fredericksburg to Mr. Yerby's plantation where there was room for the family to enjoy a short time together.

The Yerby plantation was situated on the plains in a valley. In the distance the long chain of mountains were a mass of pale green as the trees began to show their young leaves. There was just a hint of snow left on the mountaintop and it shone bright in a warm April sun. Tom woke to the sound of a robin, just outside his window. He turned to Anna, who lay still sleeping. Just then, there was another sound from the crib across the room. Julia was making sounds. Tom could hear her as she sucked on her fist. She's hungry, he thought. He leaned over and kissed Anna. His beautiful wife whom he adored, and how he missed her!

"Good morning, dearest."

"Oh, Tom. How wonderful to wake up and find you here beside me. Do you know how much I miss you?"

"Yes, I do and do you know what it's like to be out in the middle of a battlefield and know you can't get home to your wife?"

He put his arms around her and held her close. He cherished every tender moment they would have together. There had been so few. There was this ominous feeling, deep within his breast, that the time would soon come and he would have to leave her. He wished this moment would never end and he could hold his beloved in his arms where she would be safe from harm. He dared not question God or His works but he wished this terrible war would end.

Julia had waited long enough. Her cries were no longer tolerant as she let her parents know it was breakfast time. Anna jumped up and went to the crib to pick the baby up. After she was dried and comfortable, she brought her back to the bed to nurse her. Tom looked at the two of them and thought they were the most beautiful ladies in the world!

Portrait of "Stonewall" Jackson by Minnes (1863)

Chapter 15

The peace and quiet of the morning was abruptly ended as the thunder of cannon shook the windowpanes in the bedroom. Tom jumped up and looked out of the window. The great Rappahannock was in the distance and he could see the Federal army crossing it.

"Anna, here come the Yankees! Get dressed as quickly as you can and pack your things. You and Julia will have to get away as quickly as possible. I'll call Sparks and have him escort you back."

Before he could finish dressing, he heard someone running across the front porch then climb the stairs to their room. A knock on the door came soon after.

"What is it?"

"General Early's adjutant wishes to see General Jackson."

"Tell him, I'll be there in ten minutes."

He hastily finished and went out to Early's tent. Within a few minutes he was back to see about Anna.

"We must hurry and get you out. The Federals have 138,000 of their troops coming this way. You must go southward immediately."

I had received the General's call and was ready to take Anna, the baby and the maid back to North Carolina. We just made it out of there before the bullets began flying. The General put her and the baby in the buggy, kissed them goodbye, and I took the reins as we sped toward Richmond where she would catch her train.

Jackson no longer had time to think about his family. He had to get a message to Lee who came directly to Jackson's headquarters.

"Hooker has brought his men across the river and they are passing west of Fredericksburg going toward a place known as Chancellorsville. I understand it's a crossroads of the trails in the Wilderness and has one single brick house in a clearing of about one hundred acres."

They discussed the possible assault, then Lee gave Jackson orders to go through the Spotsylvania Wilderness toward Chancellorsville. They would move on May first. He told Jackson to take General McLaws and the three brigades Longstreet had left behind. Early's division would hold the river front but the army must not fight with the river bank at its back!

Just after midnight on May first, Jackson put on his new uniform and ordered his troops to move out. General Rodes and his men led, with A.P. Hill and Trimble's old division, under General Colstom in their rear. By eight in the morning, Jackson had his men settled near Chancellorsville. The Yankees expected Jackson to move in and begin fighting but they were wrong. Three hours passed and no shots had been fired. They could wait no longer. At eleven twenty the first gun of the battle of Chancellorsville sounded. McLaws had been caught up in a musket fight and Jackson's men had encountered the enemy. The battle was beginning to build up.

Stuart sent Jackson a message that he was three miles below Chancellorsville and would close in on the flank and help all he could. Jackson scratched a reply on the back of the original note.

"I trust that God will grant us a great victory. Keep lines closed on Chancellorsville."

He met Jeb Stuart about four o'clock and they rode to a point where they could get a clear look over the lines to Chancellorsville. The lines of the enemy were in plain sight. It would be hard to storm Hooker's position. There would be some serious fighting as Lee had a force of 60,000 and Hooker had 130,00. Lee went back but before leaving the plans to Jackson, he told Stuart to cover Jackson with his cavalry.

Jackson rode over to the campfire where his friend Reverend Lacy sat. He was Jackson's chief chaplain and was thoroughly familiar with the area.

"Is there a road where I could attack the Yankees in the flank?"

"Yes, there are two or three you could use to attack their left flank."

"Show them to me on this map."

Lacy began to mark off a road but Jackson said he needed more of an area in which to maneuver. The Chaplain then mentioned a trail from Catherine Furnace into the Plank Road that was used for moving iron ore. They needed a guide and one who knew everything about the area. Chaplain Lacy said he knew just the right person and would go fetch him. We would meet him later.

Jackson was chilled to the bone. He had neither jacket or blanket and as he began shivering, one of the men went to a nearby campfire and brought him back a cup of coffee. Lee came up to talk about the attack and while Jackson was telling him about it, Lacy came back with the information about the trail. The three men leaned down by the light of the campfire and studied the map. Lee turned to Jackson and asked,

"How many men will you need?"

"All of my entire corps."

"Who will you leave with me?"

"The divisions of Anderson and McLaws."

Lee agreed to the plan and began to scratch out orders while Jackson went to prepare for the road. He rode back to his tent to get his coat and blanket, having spent the night lying on a bed of pine straw beside the campfire. Chills shook his body as he rode through the pre-dawn mist.

It was seven o'clock in the morning of May 2nd when Lee and Jackson gave their orders. The 2nd Corps had begun its march toward the flank of Hooker's army. The day was pleasant and as the march progressed, the men came out of their jackets. They took the back way through the woodland trail. Jackson remarked to General Colston "that this was a Virginia Military Institute caravan." They had at least a dozen officers who had been comrades in Lexington. As the 2nd Corps marched down the Plank Road from Fredericksburg to Orange Court House, the long lines of veterans were ordered to keep silent. No conversing or loud noises were to be allowed. Key officers and their sergeants were instructed to bayonet any soldiers who violated General Jackson's orders, and the entire column was to march rapidly with as little noise as possible. The element of surprise was to be used as a fighting factor against Hooker and his 11th Corps. Jackson's countersign was "Challenge, Liberty: Reply, Independence."

The veterans of the 2nd Corps had silently marched a number of miles through the woods but Jackson had deliberately directed the troops in such a manner as to make it appear to the Union scouts that they were retreating. By late afternoon, the troops were west of the entrenched lines of the Eleventh (11th) Union Corps, commanded by Union General Oliver O. Howard.

Hooker was puzzled about the whereabouts of Jackson. He had expected to meet him head on but it was not until noon that day that he saw the movement of Jackson's troops from his own headquarters. He spread a map on his cot and tried to decide what Jackson was doing. He could not believe it was a retreat to Richmond without a fight. Hooker sat and waited and still no Jackson! By mid afternoon, some of Hooker's lookouts and officers begged him to be aware of the movement to their right but the General only scoffed at them and asked why they were so frightened. A few minutes later, he received a message from a brigade commander saying, "a large body of the enemy is massing in my front; for God's sake, make disposition to receive him." And still Hooker did not believe him!

Jackson had ordered that when the actual attack against Hooker's 11th Corps began, all buglers were to play the "charge" signal up and down the line while every man was to go forward, bayonets attached to rifles, yelling the Rebel charge refrain as loudly as they could and running with all the speed they could muster. The more commotion and noise they made while charging the Union lines would result in more confusion and fear among the soldiers of the 11th Corps.

By late afternoon, Hooker began to smell the odor of cooking food coming from far right of his Union line. General Jackson had stopped to permit his hungry men to rest and eat supper. Most of them had not eaten all day as they tramped and plodded along the road leading to the 11th Corps troops. Hooker immediately sent out orders to his divisions to start the attack on the Confederates. Within the hour, some of Jackson's pickets had exchanged fire with the enemy. Other Federal regiments came behind them and at the sound of bugles, the ranks were driving ahead full speed. They found themselves surrounded by Yankee troops.

All troops of the 2nd Corps were now in orderly formation for the drive against Hooker's men. Stuart's cavalry was drawn up in attack formation, with each trooper prepared to draw sabers, while horse drawn artillery was moved into the higher ground ready to launch its cannonades against enemy lines. The tenseness of the moment could be felt by every soldier in the 2nd Corps. Jackson raised his eyes Heavenward, elevating his left arm straight up, beseeching his Heavenly Father for victory. His prayer was very short and in keeping with his usual supplications to his Divine Helper. The General turned to Rodes and asked him if he was ready to charge.

"Yes, Sir."

"You may go forward then."

There was a crash of muskets, a thunder of cannon, and the 2nd Corps began to run, shouting the Rebel Yell at the top of their lungs as they charged and rolled through woods. The 11th Union Corps were terrified to hear the sounds roaring through the early evening and petrified by the tremendous horde that came at them from the forest. Never in all their wildest imaginations did the Union troops imagine a sight such as they now beheld. Before them came a veritable avalanche of gray uniforms, charging with glistening bayonets and yelling the most ferocious sounds that any of them had ever heard. It was like a scene out of Dante's Inferno, only instead of devils with tails brandishing smoking pitchforks, the Confederates came at them with cold steel bayonets and a fury that could not be withstood.

General Howard knew that he had never witnessed such a catastrophe as Jackson crushed Hooker's flank before his very eyes. Holding the high ground, just a little after six in the evening, Jackson ordered a second charge which carried the men forward to Dowall's Tavern. He galloped through the forest shouting,

"Press Forward, Press Forward!"

He stopped now and then to turn his eyes toward Heaven, asking God for His blessing. He did this not once but so often that his men commented about it. As he passed men who had fallen, he would stop and pray over them. This went on until the troops of the 2nd Corps had to stop because of darkness. No night attack was planned since the enemy was moving and no Federals lay between Jackson's lines and the vital heights of Fairview.

A change of plans came about when the moon came up and the General could see where they were going. The pressure of the fighting had been very intense and while the 2nd Corps smashed and destroyed the Union 11th Corps, the price they paid was fearful. Jackson turned to Lane and told him he was also to push on. The commanding general was now between the battle line of Lane's brigade and his own line of skirmishers. A steady chopping and hacking could be heard, leading Jackson to believe that the Federals were fortifying themselves.

It was between 8:00 and 9:00 P.M. that Jackson rode forward to reconnoiter. The staff with him was aware of the darkness and the dangers that lurked therein. As the little party turned toward its own lines, a friendly regiment mistook them for enemy cavalry. Shots rang out and men and horses went down. The General was among the first ones hit. Spurring his horse across the road to his right, he was met by a second volley from the right company of Pender's North Carolina brigade. Jackson was hit by three shots; one penetrated the palm of his right hand; a second hit around the wrist of his left arm and exited through the hand; the third went through the left arm about half way from shoulder to elbow, splintering the large bone of the upper arm. His horse caromed from the line of fire into the wild brush and the General's face and forehead were badly scratched. As he could not control his hold on the bridle rein, he reeled in the saddle and was caught by Captain Milbourne of the Signal Corps as he was about to fall.

General Pender who was on the scene, cried out;

"Oh, General, I hope you are not seriously wounded. I will have to retire to reform my troops as they are pretty well broken by this fire and shot!"

Although in great pain and semi-conscious, Jackson firmly said, "You must hold your ground, you must hold your ground, sir!"

The firing around Jackson and his party became more intense and in the darkness the noise of the night and confusion that ensued seemed like it would never end. They laid Jackson on the ground as General Hill rode up and leaped from his horse.

"Are you much hurt, General?"

"I think I am. All my wounds are from my own men."

Hill examined Jackson and found that his left arm was shattered at the elbow. One bullet had gone in his left wrist and hand and another had lodged in the palm of his right hand. As General Hill bandaged Jackson's wounds as best he could, the shooting raged all around. Young officers crouched around Jackson trying to shield him from the flying bullets. Men were sent to obtain a litter and it was obvious that the General was bleeding profusely and time was of the essence for medical help to save him. When the litter was found, the General was lifted carefully and placed on it laying on his back. Willing hands and arms lifted the litter but just as they started forward, one of the bearers was hit by a stray bullet and the litter fell with Jackson hitting the ground on his left side where his arm had been shattered. The pain and agony caused by the fall increased the necessity for speedy action in having a doctor tend to the General as fast as possible. A messenger was sent out to locate Dr. Hunter McGuire, chief surgeon of the 2nd Corps, Jackson's personal physician. The wounded General was put on another litter and taken through the woods to a point where the now located Dr. McGuire met them with an ambulance. As Dr. McGuire knelt down he examined Jackson quickly and said,

"I hope you are not hurt much, General."

"Doctor, I feel like I'm badly injured. I fear I'm dying."

The doctor looked at the wounds again and then had the men put him into an ambulance. Colonel Crutchfield was already in there, badly wounded. He was suffering and as he moaned, Jackson listened and then called the doctor.

"Please stop the ambulance and do something for Colonel Crutchfield."

"We will be at the hospital soon. I can't do anything more for either of you until we get there."

The ambulance rocked and jolted its way along the rough road, with the General and Colonel moaning and groaning through the entire ride. At the home of Reverend Melzi Chancellor, Jackson was examined by Dr. McGuire who instructed the ambulance drivers and orderlies to proceed immediately on the three mile ride with Jackson to the field hospital overlooking Wilderness Run. Arriving at the field hospital, the General was given some morphine to help ease the pain, and put to bed. He slept for some time and when he awoke, Dr. McGuire told him about his wounds.

"General, your wounds in your arm and hand are bad. We can't repair the damage. The only thing left to do is to amputate the arm before you get an infection.''

"Do what you must, doctor!''

Dr. McGuire told the General that chloroform would be administered and the wounds probed. The bullet in the right hand was removed without any problems. At approximately 2:15 AM, his left arm was amputated by Dr. McGuire and staff. The operation appeared to be successful, the left arm being amputated about two inches below the shoulder. Jackson's chaplain, Beverly Tucker Lacy arranged for the burial of Jackson's amputated arm in the Lacy family cemetery at the plantation known as Ellwood. The cemetery was located not far from the Wilderness Tavern, where the General's left arm was removed early on the morning of May 3, 1863. There, in the middle of the field is a small stand of cedars surrounded by a kneehigh, post and rail fence, known as the Ellwood Cemetery. J. Horace Lacy, brother of Chaplain Beverly Tucker Lacy, represented the Lacy family who owned this burial plot at the time the General's arm was interred. A simple solitary stone marks the spot where the remains of Jackson's left arm were placed.

The question of "Stonewall" Jackson's recovery was paramount in the minds of General Lee and the 2nd Corps of the Army of Northern Virginia. His smashing victory over Hooker had imbued the South with an enthusiasm not seen since the days of First Manassas. His name was on the lips of all Southerners and the newspapers gave a wide press to the hero of Chancellorsville and the Commander in Chief, General Robert E. Lee. Everyone prayed with fervor for his rapid recovery and continued brilliant military leadership!

Later that morning, following Dr. McGuire's surgery, Jackson awakened from a drugged sleep, feeling somewhat shaky and in pain from his throbbing wounds, and talked with Sandie Pendleton and other officers about the battle with Hooker and arrangements for Sunday services. Having been advised that Hill had also been wounded, the General named Jeb Stuart as leader of the 2nd Corps and then listened as he was read a note from General Robert E. Lee. Late in the afternoon, a messenger from General Stuart brought word that Jeb did not know what Jackson's plans were for continuing the fight against Hooker's army and wanted to know what orders for the day would be. The General told the messenger to tell Stuart "to go on and do what he thinks best.''

Orders came from General Lee that General Jackson be moved to a safer spot. Jackson was asked if he had any preference, and he recalled the hospitality and warmth of the Chandler family at Guinea Station from the prior year. On Monday morning, May 4th, Jackson was lifted into an army ambulance for the approximate 25 mile ride to the Chandler house. Jedediah Hotchkiss arranged for some engineers and the Quartermaster to ascertain that the Brock road leading to the area of the Chandler house was clear. Quartermaster Harman, very heavily involved in moving teams of material, munitions, food and guns for the 2nd Corps, personally undertook to see to it that his teamsters had sidelined any and all equipment items that were not absolutely essential to the fighting at that moment. His affection and regard for his beloved General's welfare went far beyond the bounds of his duties as Quartermaster. None of his rough and tough bully boys were to impede or block any of the roads that Jackson would have to pass, and if necessary the toughest man in the Quartermaster Corps, Harman himself, would personally knock over any man in his command who stood in the General's way. Although forbidden to make any noises, Harman's men let out a tremendous cheer when Jackson's ambulance passed through them on the normally crowded road!

Word had been passed to all company and regimental commanders as well as the troops that General Jackson had survived the amputation and would be transferred by ambulance to the Chandler house for recuperation. All commanders were ordered to insure the route that the ambulance would take as requested by General Robert E. Lee and that the road would be cleared of all military outside of emergency situations. Noise would be held at an absolute minimum so that the General was not disturbed during his ambulance transfer. Dr. McGuire, Chaplain Lacy and Lieutenant James Power Smith rode with the General. All along the route, seasoned veterans of all ranks removed their hats or caps and saluted as the ambulance carrying their beloved commander drove by. A fervent prayer for his recovery was on the lips of the men of the 2nd Corps, as all along the ambulance's route men and women rushed forward with food, flowers and good wishes. Most were in tears and praying for his recovery. General Jackson withstood the trip well when he arrived at Chandler's the main house was full with the wounded from the battle. Chaplain Lacy's wife, Beverly arranged with the Chandlers that Jackson be placed in the little office building to insure privacy and quiet. The Chandlers quickly arranged to change everything around in the office building so that Jackson and his attendants would have all the comforts needed to insure a rapid recovery. The General arrived around 8:00 P.M. that evening. His pain had almost stopped and he was beginning to talk to the people around him. He could still hear the battle raging around him; the guns were not silent, indicating that the fighting was still going on. He listened to the reports coming in and when they mentioned the ''Stonewall Brigade,'' he kept saying, ''Good, good!''

House where "Stonewall" Jackson died in 1863.

The next morning, May 5th, as Dr. McGuire changed the bandages, the wounds looked like they were improving. Jackson ate a hearty breakfast and later, Chaplain Lacy led the daily prayer service. Jackson had told his aides that he wanted Lacy to conduct a daily prayer service each morning that he was confined at Chandler's. The arrangement in the office building was just right as Lieutenant James P. Smith occupied a room in the upstairs section, one room was used by the doctor and his staff and the kitchen lorded over by his body servant, Jim. Dr. McGuire also used a couch in the General's room so that he could be near him in case of any emergency during his recovery.

The Richmond Whig, in an editorial dedicated to "Lee and Jackson," said on May 9, 1863:

JACKSON WOUNDED

"His left arm gone, his right hand maimed, the lion hearted Jackson rests in the house of a friend, cheerful, resigned to the will of that Providence in which he so firmly trusts, patiently biding his time. General Lee's sublime tribute to his services in the late battles, his profound and sincere sympathy for his sufferings, leaves us at a loss which to love and admire most—the author or the receiver of the letter, in which this magnanimity and manly sorrows are conveyed. "How gladly would I have borne, in my own person, the serious loss you have sustained, for to you and to you alone is due the victory we have achieved." To this effect is Lee's letter. Who is not proud to live in the same day and belong to the same race with such men. It is an honor to breathe the air they breathe. Together, they make up a measure of glory which no nation under Heaven ever surpassed. Other great leaders we have, to whom unstinted praise is due and everywhere gladly accorded; but the rays of their fame coverage and accumulate but to add to the dazzling splendor that illuminates the names of Lee and Jackson.

The central figure of this war is, beyond all question, that of Robert E. Lee. His, the calm, broad military intellect that reduced the chaos after Donelson to form and order. But Jackson is the motive power that executes, with the rapidity of lightening, all that Lee can plan. Lee is the exponent of Southern power of command; Jackson, the expression of its faith in God and in itself, its terrible energy, its enthusiasm and daring, its unconquerable will, its concept of danger and fatigue, its capacity to smite, as with bolts of thunder, the cowardly and cruel foe that would tramp under its foot its liberty and its religion.

We need have no fears for Jackson. He is no accidental manifestation of the powers of faith and courage. He came not by chance in this day and to this generation. He was born for a purpose, and not until that purpose is fulfilled will his great soul take flight. Of this, no one is more sure than himself. In this conviction, he rests serenely, awaiting the healing of his wounds; willing more to hear the wild cheers of his men as he rides to the front; or if that be denied him, content to retire from the field, a maimed, humble, Christian man. Civil honor, were it the highest in the gift of the country, could not add one cubit to the stature of his glory.

Even should he die, his fiery and unquailing spirit would survive in his men. He has infused into them that which cannot die. The leader who succeeds him, be he whom he may, will be impelled, as by supernatural impulse, to emulate his matchless deeds. Jackson's men will demand to be led in "Stonewall Jackson's way." The leader who will not or cannot comply with that demand, must drop the baton quickly. Jackson's corps will be led forever by the memory of its great chieftain.

But Jackson will not die. He will be unable to resume command for some weeks, and that is a great loss to us, for time is precious now. His arm, no Yankee loss can ever repay. The paring of his little finger nail is of more value than all the hosts of Northmen in the field. Truly, the victory was dearly bought.''

Chapter 16

Jackson was fairly comfortable at Guinea Station. He kept up his interests in the fighting and usually spent some of his time discussing theological matters with one of his aides, Lieutenant James Power Smith. Quoting from his favorite verse, "All things work together for good for those who love the Lord," taken from Romans 8:28, he engaged Powers in an exchange of ecclesiastical interpretations which stimulated his mind and warmed his fondness for the young man who reminded Jackson of his earlier years of youth. The pain in his right hand persisted; the left shoulder and side ached constantly, despite the draining and healing of the operated area. Dr. McGuire, his aides and Jim, did what they could for the General, changing the bandages often, putting cooling cloths on his stomach and sides and trying to make him as comfortable as possible. Pain killers were administered often but the General refused to take any whiskey as a relief liquid. He did eat with fairly good appetite. Jim, his body servant saw to it that Jackson had all the things he liked, prepared and served in the manner that the General appreciated. Although Jackson was never a gourmet, the food he enjoyed the most was simple and usually home-style. Jim saw to it that he got plenty of what he liked.

Mrs. Jackson, staying in Richmond with a friend, Mrs. Hoge, was advised on May 6th of the extent of the General's wounds, and decided to come to Guinea Station with little Julia and her nurse Hetty. The General had a bad night, became nauseated and asked his body servant, Jim, to put a wet towel on him. Dr. McGuire was not awakened, having become exhausted watching over Jackson and not getting any sleep. The pain that developed in Jackson's side, worsened, and when McGuire awakened and checked him out, he realized that pneumonia had set in.

When Mrs. Jackson and Julia arrived at the Chandler building where the General was, her husband's condition had deteriorated from the previous evening. He was in great pain and his breathing labored.

The General slept fitfully. He seemed to be holding his own but not much improved. His conversation during the day, brief as it was, expressed confidence that he would live and still believed that his Heavenly Father had a lot more work for him to do on earth before he was called to God's Eternal Paradise!

By the next day, Saturday, May 9th he was considerably weaker but not incoherent. He said to Dr. McGuire, "I see from the number of physicians that you think my condition dangerous but I thank God, if it is His will, that I am ready to go." He wanted to see Julia and talk with her if he could. She was brought in and rallied his spirits by her smile, few words and delightful attention to her father. Jackson wept with joy as he held her hand as they talked. Anna, too, received his attention while she was in the room. She read Bible passages to him and when he asked her to sing something, difficult as it was for her to do under the circumstances, she sang the lines of the 51st Psalm, "Show pity, Lord; O Lord, forgive." By the time she finished the song, she was inundated by tears and her emotions overflowed with love and sympathy for Tom. He was dying and there was nothing she or anyone could do to help him!

Sunday, May 10th dawned bright and early for the Lord's Day. Dr. McGuire had already advised Anna that the General would not live out the day and that she should expect the worst to happen not later than that afternoon. The General was then advised by his beloved that this day he would be taken by his Heavenly Father and Jackson's reply was that "it will be my gain to be translated to Heaven." He talked with Anna, advising upon his death, she should return to her home, and see to it that he was buried in Lexington. His condition worsened as the day wore on. Sandie Pendelton entered the room and the General asked him who was preaching at headquarters that day. Pendelton told him that the entire army as well as all the people were praying for him. Jackson thanked him and mentioned that he always wanted to be taken on the Lord's Day and that his wish be fulfilled by his God.

As the day wore on, the entire hospital area became aware of the dying moments of the great commanding General of the 2nd Corps of the Army of Northern Virginia. A pall descended on the perimeter in which was located the Chandler building wherein the General lay. Officers and men alike kept a deathwatch vigil, as periodically eyes turned to the room in which Jackson was breathing his last. A veritable powder keg of deep emotion was about to burst from the hearts and minds of the people who loved him most!

The clock opposite the General ticked on as moment by moment his life ebbed away. Anna kept reading the Bible aloud as Dr. McGuire administered to the patient. Jim, his loyal and devoted body servant stood by the doorway while Lieutenant James Power Smith, watched his commander, never once lifting his eyes from the breath laboring bearded face. The General began to mumble in between rattling breaths, talking of battle actions, Anna and Julia, Laura, Uncle Will, and his staff. In his delirium, he began to shout, "Order A. P. Hill to prepare for action! Pass the infantry to the front rapidly…tell Major Hawkes to…have Jeb Stuart…" and then with his final breath as though he saw the Heavens open up to him, he said, "Let us cross over the river and rest under the shade of the trees!" The time on the clock facing the General was 3:15 P.M. The life and career of Lt. General Thomas Jonathan "Stonewall" Jackson was over!

A message was sent by telegraph to Richmond;

"General Jackson died at fifteen minutes past three this afternoon."

How simple and appropriate was this final message about a man who had given his all for the country and nation which he held so close and loved so much! Now, history and an adoring people would tender him the kudos and praise he deserved for duty, honor and devotion to a cause which became his life and ultimately his untimely death!

Anna went into the parlor of the Chandler house on Monday morning, May 11th. Her beloved had been gone since 3:15 P.M. the day before, and already she knew not how to live without him. She walked up to the casket and looked at him once again. Someone had dressed him in civilian clothes, wrapping a blue military overcoat around him. His wooden coffin, covered with spring flowers, gave a peaceful appearance of rest for the great General. She reached over and touched his face; his appearance was normal although there was a waxy sheen to him which the undertakers sent from Richmond had to apply in order to best display the strong and remarkable profile of the great military leader. She turned then to join the people who were honored to accompany her and the General to Richmond.

Since I had been the aide of Jackson throughout his many campaigns, I was given a place of honor with the family. We solemnly walked to a special railroad care which had been reserved for us. His casket was borne by an honor guard made up of selected veterans of the "Stonewall Brigade" and placed in the car in which he would ride. All officers and men stationed around Chandler hospital came to attention as the honor guard carried the General to the train, the only sound to be heard was the shuffling of feet and the steps taken in transferring the body from the horse-drawn hearse into the black bedecked train carriage. Anna, Julia, the nurse Hetty, Mrs. Hoge, the friend who had come from Richmond, and Mrs. Chandler, got on first. Those following were Sandie Pendelton, two aides, James Morrison, Lieutenant James P. Smith, and Captain Kyd Douglas, Major J. W. Hawks, the commisary officer, Chaplain Lacy, Major D. B. Bridgford, Provost Marshal, Dr. David Tucker and Doctor Smith, a consultant of Dr. McGuire. The men of the "Stonewall" brigade had wanted to go but General Lee would not let them. He wrote a note to Captain Kyd Douglas saying the Yankees were showing signs of movement and it was too dangerous to have his best men leave. He knew that General Jackson would not have wanted them to neglect their duty. There were other component and significant parts of the 2nd Corps (officers and men) who out of love and affection for their dead commander, sought permission to represent their respective regiments and divisions at the General's funeral in Richmond. They too were refused permission by the headquarters of General Lee on the same grounds as was refused to the "Stonewall" brigade. As the train steamed out of the Guinea Station, people who lived in the environs waved and bade a tearful farewell to their beloved "Stonewall."

The train traveled forty-five miles to Richmond. It took hours and while the weather was unbearably hot, those on board the sad journey suffered terribly. Anna could not bear the thought of facing the teeming throngs of people who waited at the Richmond train station and all along the way. They stopped the train so that she and her party of family and friends could get off and take a lesser traveled route to the Richmond Mansion. As the train moved into the station, the coffin was removed and the local honor guard began the slow march to the Capitol Square. The streets were silent as bowed heads of thousands were seen.

The coffin was moved into the large reception room. Outside, the bells tolled until sundown as a vast multitude remained in the Square grieving for their hero. Anna was in full mourning dress as she made her way to the reception room to find that the lid of the coffin was permanently sealed and she could only see her beloved through glass.

On Tuesday, May 12th, all offices and businesses were closed in Richmond as a sign of respect and mourning for the General. At 11:00 that morning, the General was placed in a horse drawn hearse, led by a military escort and followed by the Public Guard and Camp Guard on a funeral march. Longstreet's First Corps marched alongside the hearse, while four generals who had served under Jackson, acted as pallbearers. Among the generals marching and paying homage to Jackson were: Elzy, Garnett, George H. Steuart, Ewell, Kemper, Corse, John H. Winder and Commodore French Forest. Chief Marshal of the funeral procession was General George W. Randolph. Just behind the hearse came Jim, leading Jackson's horse with stirrups reversed, and recuperating veterans of the "Stonewall" brigade located in Richmond at the time.

Behind the military came the President and Vice President of the Confederacy, who rode in a carriage; behind them the government officials walking two by two with Secretary Benjamin and Secretary Seddon in the lead. Governor Letcher was in the forefront of the Virginia group, city officials and prominent citizens in a procession almost a mile long. The long procession looped around the city, carrying the General through long lines of people, then back to Capitol Square to the Confederate House of Representatives where they placed the coffin on a catafalque covered with white linen in front of the Speaker's chair. The hall was draped in mourning and the General lay in state so the people could pay tribute to him. Some 20,000 persons streamed by that afternoon.

Anna sat in a waiting room outside the hall, with her family and friends around her. Her brother, Major W. W. Morrison, was there from North Carolina as was Mrs. William N. Page, a hometown friend. Reverend T. V. Moore sat with her and read parts of the Bible aloud, including the 14th chapter of the Book of John. The day was hard on everyone, especially on me, as I sat there thinking of our life and times together.

Memories surged within me and I harked back to the days of the Mexican War and my first contacts with the young Lieutenant from West Point. How resolute and determined he was—his desire to get ahead and be promoted was ever with him! His bravery and heroics in countless battles presaged a future that had limitless boundaries. With all his ambition and logical approaches to the problems he encountered, he persevered and accomplished in life, short as it was for him, more things than most men living much longer lives ever did. His faith in his God was always unshakeable and his path led him unerringly through preordination and predestination! VMI was just another period in his life cycle, but what he accomplished with the raw material he had there filled the military books of the South as well as the North. Abraham Lincoln and the military giants of the Northern states would never forget the impact he made on them with his ability to outfight, outthink, and decisively beat back their overwhelming numbers and mount crushing but devastating attacks of his own. At a moment like this, it was difficult to realize that this military genius, lay in his coffin lifeless while his devoted followers and admirers honored him with what practically amounted to a national funeral. The genius of Jackson would soon not be forgotten and I, Caleb Joshua Sparks, had the enviable honor of having shared so much with him. Those around him were elevated by his brilliance and life was better for everyone associated with this God fearing man. It was only right that he now return to his Heavenly Father who had reserved his room some 39 years previously!

On May 13th, Wednesday, the coffin was moved from the Capitol back to the Governor's Mansion. At 7:00 it was carried to the railroad station and placed on a train for the trip to Gordonsville. Later, a change was made to an Orange and Alexandria railroad car which would take them to Lynchburg. There they changed to the canal packet, Marshall. They moved slowly through the canal toward Lexington, reaching the General's home the evening of the 14th.

A battalion of VMI cadets met the General's body and Anna had the sad chore of stepping off the boat and facing the good people of Lexington. A large crowd of fellow citizens accompanied the cadets as they carried his body up the hill to the classroom where he taught for ten years at VMI. The cadets stood straight as bayonets as they guarded him through the night with every man at VMI vying for the honor and privilege of being a member of the group that performed this sad duty. Jackson, the professor of natural philosophy and artillery tactics for ten years at VMI was now home as the heroic military genius of countless battles! S. B. Hannah, a student at VMI, was the Officer of the Day, when the body of General Jackson was brought in to the Institute and wrote the following excerpted letter to his mother about his experiences:

May 17, 1863

"Dear Mother,

I am very sorry to say that I have deferred writing to you so long, but John wrote a few days back and I concluded that one from me would be more agreeable if it was postponed a while longer. As to what has transpired since you received the last from the Institute I know of little except the burial of Generals Jackson and Paxton. For the last week we have been doing nothing worthy of note that is in the way of studying except acting as a funeral escort to the honored dead of our country. *Noble occupation* for a body of young men able to fight their country's battles. Do not think me endeavoring to deprecate the honor attached to the burial of such noble heroes, for while I lament and hang my head in shame at the idea of not having the privilege and honor of calling myself one of the veterans of Jackson's Corps, still it will be ever gratifying and pleasant in after years for me to recall the solemn scenes through which I passed in the last week, namely the burial of Generals Jackson and Paxton.

I was Officer of the Day when the body of General Jackson was brought in Barracks, no military escort accompanied him from Richmond, only a few citizens, among them the Governor. His body was said to be embalmed, but of no avail. Decomposition had already taken place, in consequence of which his face was not exposed to view as the features were said not to be natural. The coffin was a perfect flower bed and under that which was presented to his wife by the President, the first new Confederate flag ever made. His body was placed in his old section room which will remain draped for six months.

General Smith then requested that none of the flowers should be removed from the coffin which was an impossibility although I had a Sentinel guarding the remains. Still the Sentinels would remove things for themselves and of course they were afraid to inform on others for fear of being caught at it themselves. I did not think it right to take what others had placed there as a memorial of their love and esteem for our beloved Jackson, although I would prize a trophy like that the highest imaginable. Still as it had been entrusted to me to see that all was kept right, so long as his body was under my charge, I couldn't conscientiously take any of the flowers when I knew that every Cadet was afraid to let me see him take or touch the body.

He only remained in Barracks one day and night. He was buried on Friday, May 15th. Dr. White preached his funeral, the old gentleman seemed and I know he was deeply affected, for from all accounts the General took quite an active part in the Church and was the founder of the Colored Sunday School and the main stay of it as long as he was in Lexington.

I am compelled to put out my lights—so good bye and my love to all and Aunt Charlotte's family.

Your son,
S. B. Hannah"

In time some of the Cadets who were privileged to perform this trust became famous but all regarded this service as one of the most honored and impressive experiences of their life. The officers and Cadets of the Institute were then ordered to wear the usual badge of mourning for a period of thirty days and the lecture room in which his coffin lay was draped in mourning for six months. The Cadet Battery which Jackson commanded for ten years was ordered to honor his memory by half-hour guns on the morrow from sunrise to sunset.

The funeral procession moved from the Institute on Friday morning, May 15th at 10:00 A.M. The funeral escort was commanded by Major S. Strip, a commandant of Cadets, a former pupil of General Jackson and a gallant officer who had served with him in his Valley Campaign, as Major of the 21st Virginia Regiment. The escort was composed as follows:

1. The Cadet Battalion.
2. Battery of Artillery of 4 pieces, the same battery he had for ten years commanded as Professor of Artillery and which had also served with him at 1st Manassas in the Stonewall Brigade.
3. A company of the original Stonewall Brigade composed of members of different companies of the Brigade and commanded by Captain A. Hamilton, bearing the flag of the "Liberty Hall Volunteers."
4. A company of convalescent officers and soldiers of the army.
5. A squadron of cavalry was all that was needed to complete the escort prescribed by Army Regulations. This squadron opportunity made its appearance before the procession moved from the Church. The Squadron was a part of Sweeny's battalion of Jenkin's command, and many of its members were from the General's native Northwestern Virginia.
6. The Clergy.
7. The body enveloped in the new Confederate flag and covered with flowers, was borne on a caisson of the Cadet Battery, draped in mourning.

The pall bearers were as follows:

William White and Professor J. L. Campbell,
representing the Elders of the Lexington
Presbyterian Church.

William C. Lewis and Colonel S. McDaniel Reid,
County Magistrates.

Professors J. J. White and C. J. Harris,
Washington College

S. McDonald Moore and John W. Fuller,
Franklin Society

Monument signifying where Jackson fell.

George W. Adams and Robert T. White,
Town Council

Judge J. W. Brockenbro and Joseph G. Steele,
Confederate District Court

Dr. H. H. McGuire and Captain F. W. Henderson,
Confederate States Army

Reverend W. McElwee and John Hamilton,
Bible Society of Rockridge

8. The family and personal staff of General Jackson.
9. The Governor of Virginia, G. A. Henry, Confederate State Senator from Tennesseee, the sergeant at arms of the Confederate States Senate and members of the City of Richmond council.
10. Faculty and Officers of the Virginia Military Institute.
11. Elders and Deacons of the Lexington Presbyterian Church of which Church General Jackson was a Deacon.
12. Professors and students of Washington College.
13. Franklin Society.
14. Citizens.

The funeral service was held in the Presbyterian Church in Lexington after the Cadets of V.M.I. had led the procession, marching as eight companies which were made up of a regiment of escort, more veterans of the Stonewall Brigade and two companies of cavalry. Behind the caisson drawn by four horses and on which was carried the mortal remains of General Jackson marched all the honorary pall bearers and groups paying homage to the fallen hero. The solemnity of the occasion was marked by the tremendous outpouring of grief from all those present in the streets.

There, in the midst of a sobbing group, one figure caught my eye. A woman dressed in black, with long shining blonde curls cascading out from under a black veil which covered her face held a long stemmed rose in her hand. She kissed the rose and threw it out over the caisson as the cortege passed. I knew it was Neda, paying her last respects!

As we entered the Church, Dr. White stood in the pulpit while the choir sang the hymn "How Blest And Righteous When He Dies!" Then, Reverend James B. Ramsey of Lynchburg prayed and Dr. White followed with the reading of the Fifteenth Chapter of First Corinthians and spoke of his dear friend, General Stonewall Jackson in a very personal manner. The Church service closed with a beautiful prayer given by Reverend William F. Junkin. Although the services were simple and touching, they were most appropriate for the hero who was being afforded the greatest honor his countrymen could give him. The funeral procession moved on to the cemetery at the top of the hill. There, while cannon boomed a final salute of requiem and honor for the dead, Lieutenant General Thomas Jonathan "Stonewall" Jackson was put to his everlasting rest!

The grief and loss of Jackson was universal throughout the South. Every paper came out with strong emotional expressions regarding the irreplaceable loss of the great and magnificent leader who was second only to Lee in the hearts of his countrymen. It seemed impossible for the people to believe that the General was gone forever!

EPILOGUE

Anna Jackson and daughter Julia returned to live in North Carolina at her father's home. I took Jim, the General's loyal and trusted body servant back to my farm in Virginia and turned Old Sorrel over to Anna's family so that he could live out his remaining years roaming their pastures, free from the cannister and shot and away from the terrible sounds of battle. After I returned to my quarters at Chancellorsville, the War Department in Richmond granted me a leave of absence which I used in an extended visit to my farm at Forestville. During my leave and while on my farm, I sustained a crippling injury while doing some chores and the Army discharged me from the service. Thus, I never returned to active duty.

Now that I had a surfeit of time on hand, my feelings for General Jackson expressed the very deep sense of personal loss which I as his aide and personal friend felt. His life was a pattern of morality, religious servitude to God, loyalty and affection for family, unwaivering faith plus devotion to duty and sacrifice for his country. He chose to live a life which was in keeping with his ideals regardless of what his neighbors and fellowmen thought of his enigmatic ways. His honesty and convictions in maintaining relations with all people were never challenged. He could be gentle and kind, and yet on the other hand, in carrying out his position as a brilliant military leader, he could be tough, non-yielding and absolutely stubborn. Such was the man who never displayed a two-faced visage to his fellow officers, colleagues or peers.

He chose to give his all for the cause in which he believed and will go down in history as an inspiration to the citizens of our country, both North and South. Generations of future Americans will look back and conclude that great leaders will continue to come and go as the years pass on into the centuries, but the likes of a "Stonewall" Jackson will be few and far between!

In the pantheon of great Americans, Jackson will stand out as that exception who will forever be remembered as a man who loved the cause of freedom and died a hero's death while holding to his firm convictions that Almighty God would lead all men to the peace and enjoyment of a better life! His imprint and legacy to the South and to the American concept of life, liberty and the pursuit of happiness, is an indelible treasure that will never be erased by time. Truly, if any one deserved to "cross over the river and rest under the shade of the trees," Jackson was that man.